With her there will be no regrets.

Book 2 in The Liquor Cabinet series
Liquor has never been so disturbingly saucy

I had been fooled once. Misled and lied to. There was no going back from that. The fact I was so easily tricked and betrayed gnawed at my bones, and it was causing me to self-destruct.

I've put up walls around me the size of Texas, and no one will break them down—not even the pretty waitress with doe eyes, and a warm smile.

Sav is there whenever I decide to wallow in regret, a bottle and a glass my only company. And even though I'm determined to not let anyone in, Sav somehow worms her way into my life without even trying.

Every time I look into her eyes, I can see there's something different about her. She's an enigma, her life a mystery I want to solve.

It's only when the devil from her past comes knocking that I realise how much danger she's really in. Her life is threatened, and it's up to me to protect her.

If that means I have to walk through hell twice, then that's what I'll do.

Tequila Healing, book 2 in the Liquor Cabinet series.

Edited by Karen Hrdlicka, Barren Acres Editing

Cover design by Tash Drake, Outlined with Love Designs

 Created with Vellum

WARNING

This book contains content this is not suitable for persons under 18. Drugs, alcohol, assault, torture, sexual content, including a threesome and lots of course language are included in this book.

If these subjects offend, then this book probably isn't for you.

AUTHOR'S NOTE

Some of the chapters repeat themselves, as they are given from both points of views. I have added extra and tweaked them, so that these scenes are not exactly the same.

The legal drinking age is Australia is 18.

This book contains Australian slang as it is set in Australia and uses Australian spelling.

Here is a glossary to help you out:

Missus – Wife/Girlfriend/Partner
Arvo – Afternoon
Headjob – Blowjob
Undies – Panties
Franga – Condom
Singlet – Tank
Trackies – Track pants

Thongs – Flip Flops
Hinterland – Mountains
Esky – Cool Box/ Cooler
Ambo – Ambulance Officer
Up the duff – pregnant
Obs – vitals – blood pressure, temp etc.
Maccas – McDonald's
Bottle-O – Liquor store
Mines – that is mine
Brewski's – alcoholic beverages

THE LIQUOR CABINET SERIES

Liquor has never been so disturbingly saucy

ALSO BY DL GALLIE

THE CASTAWAY GROVE COLLECTION
Love has arrived in the Grove

Oasis
Unequivocal Love - Coming 13th October
Five Words - Coming January 2020
I've Loved You Since Forever - Coming April 2020

———

THE UNEXPECTED SERIES
When it comes to love, expect the unexpected

The Unexpected Gift
The Unexpected Letter
The Unexpected Package
The Unexpected Connection

coming November 2019

———

STAND ALONES
Out of Nowhere
Antecedent
Seven Nights

Titanic Tales, a charity anthology (no longer available)
Gone Coastal, a sizzling summer beach anthology
Leave Me Breathless: The Lilac Collection

For my mum,
Thank you for everything, you are the best mum that
anyone could ask for. If I am half as fantabolous of a mum
as you are, then I'm going a goodly job.
Love you long-time, mumsie XoXoX

PROLOGUE

It's my stupid dick's fault. I'm always thinking with my dick, and as a result, Kenz and Jordan nearly lost everything, including Mac and Cheese. All because of me, my dick, and a hot blonde piece of ass named Ho Bag Slutface, also known as De-Niece.

Never will I fall for another woman, too much happened last time, I can't risk it happening again.

My self-imposed dick purgatory; except for random pussy but that doesn't count, was going well until Savannah Blac got a job at my local bar, The Black Dungeon. I can't stop thinking about her. The curve of her tight ass, the way it swishes side to side as she walks, or the slight bounce of her perfect tits as she passes drinks across the bar.

Every time I close my eyes, I see her. I imagine her wavy, golden blonde locks wrapped around my fists, tugging her towards me as I sink myself balls deep into her tight pink pussy from behind. Her sapphire blue eyes sparkling under the dim bar light as I slam into her over and over, and she screams my name while I give her the best orgasm of her life. Before I take her back to my place and wake up next to her in my king-sized bed, our arms and limbs wrapped around each other, her eyes dazzling in the morning sunlight.

Shaking my head to clear those dirty sweet thoughts, I concentrate on what Jordan is saying and the tequila shooter in front of me. When I look up, I see Sav walking behind the bar after her break, and I can't help but smile. She has wormed her way into my heart, and I don't know how I feel about that.

Fuck, she's gorgeous; my dick is so hard right now. I really need to find another bar to drink at, but just the thought of not seeing her crushes my heart. Picking up the shot in front of me, I say a silent "cheers" to the world for bringing her into my life. With the next shot, I say a silent "fuck you" to the world for bring her into my life… why does the universe keep doing this to me?

Welcoming the burn of the tequila as it slides down my throat, I pick up the third shot, look to Jordan, and say, "Bottoms up!" After sinking the third shot, I signal Sav for more tequila and sambuca shots and two more beers for Jordan and me.

Seeing her smile makes me grin, but then I remember that chicks are nothing but trouble and cause nothing but strife, especially the super fucking hot ones.

Remembering that I promised myself I'll never go there again, I start to think about a naked grandma, with flabby wrinkly skin, and sagging boobs. Yeah, that works for about five seconds because Sav turns around and smiles at me; she fucking smiles and it's mesmerising. It brings back memories of our one time together. *I'm screwed*, I think to myself as I keep watching her.

Shaking my head, I again consider finding another bar to drink at, but just the thought of not seeing her crushes me; I can't do it, I'm a sucker for punishment. No, I deserve this punishment for all that has happened, this is my penance to pay.

Looking over at Jordan, I think, *how can he still be friends with me, after what's happened?* I start to think of Malt Me. I could always drink there, but everyone there knows...they know I'm partly to blame for De-Niece and all the shit that went down. They stare at me with their judgey eyes; I don't need them to add to my guilt. I already feel remorse, regret, and like shit, and any number of other words to describe feeling like an asshole fuckwit.

Looking over, I see Sav smiling and I find myself also grinning back. I realise that I only ever smile when I see her. Closing my eyes, I take a deep breath to try and shake those thoughts from entering my mind, but I can't. Savannah Blac is the most beautiful woman in the world. There's nowhere else I would rather drink, the pain from seeing her is my punishment, even though I deserve much more. Besides, I love this bar; it's my happy place.

It's simple; I just have to stop thinking about Savannah Blac, no matter how perfect she is. *Nope, nah uh, not going there...again with her, even though that night was amazing.*

Everything changed when I found the gorgeous, feisty woman broken and crying in the ally behind the bar. All bets were off, she needed me and I was more than willing to step up to the plate.

Looking down at her, I saw that she was frightened, broken, and fragile; my heart broke for her. Hearing me walk towards her, she looked up at me, with tears pouring down her cheeks. Taking a deep breath, with sad eyes, she whispered, "Please. Help me."

1

MIKE

...8 months earlier

How DID I NOT KNOW? I'M SPEECHLESS, LITERALLY speechless. My girlfriend is a monster, was a monster. I was in love, with a complete and utter psychopath. How did I not see that she was just using me, helping the enemy? How could I have been so blind? How could I not have picked up on it?

I'm such a fucking fool.

Looking back towards the house, I see them cover her body with a white sheet. Immediately, a red patch develops where her wound is, it's in the moment that I realise; I just killed De-Niece.

Holy shit, I killed someone.

Holy shit, my girlfriend was working with the enemy.

Holy shit, I killed someone.

They have just taken her body away. Officer Hamilton finishes up talking with the coroner before coming over to me, I'm still sitting in the same spot; I haven't moved a muscle. I'm in complete and utter shock, with all of the discoveries and events from today.

How did I not know? I keeping asking myself the same question over and over, and each time I have the same answer; I don't know. Our relationship keeps playing over and over in my head, trying to see if I missed the signs, but nothing pops out. Even our first meeting seems random, but I guess in hindsight, it wasn't random after all.

*...I've just finished my twenty minute warm up on the treadmill and smile when **"Numb" by Linken Park** blasts through my headphones. Carefully, I hop off the treadmill to head over to the bench press. Just as I turn around, I bump into this blonde chick, quickly reaching out, I grab her arm to stop her from tumbling onto the navy carpet. I've seen her here the last few days; well I noticed her tight, pert ass and I couldn't help but smile. Ripping my ear buds out I say, "Shit, I didn't see you there."*

She looks up and smiles at me. "It's fine. I probably shouldn't have been walking so close to the treadmills anyways."

Her smile goes straight to my dick; I haven't felt like this since last week when I hooked up with what's her face from the bank. Shaking my head, I think to myself that I don't want her to leave, her smile is beautiful, it lights up her face. "Well, actually I should be apologising to you. After all, I am the one who bumped into you. I'm Mike."

"I'm De-Niece." She reaches out her hand to shake mine, and she smiles at me again. I take her hand, it's silky soft, and I imagine her wrapping her delicate fingers

around my cock, stroking it up and down, before she leans forward and sucks.

She tries to pull her hand back and that's when I realise that I'm still holding onto her, I quickly let go. "It was nice to meet you, Mike, I might see you around." She steps around me, turning back and winking at me before she heads towards the locker rooms.

De-Niece and I run into each other at the gym several times, over the next few weeks, before she finally asks me out. I'd decided that I wasn't going to go there because I really like this gym, and I didn't want to fuck up...for a change. But when she asked me out, I thought why not, she is smoking hot after all...if only I knew.

Officer Hamilton taps my shoulder and brings me back to the present. "Are you okay, Mike?"

"I...I...I don't know." Shaking my head, still staring at the house, I mumble, "I just killed someone." I look up at her. "I guess you're here to haul my ass to jail?"

"Yes, Mike, I am."

Snapping my head towards her in shock, I counter. "Fuck me, seriously?" Shaking my head as I stand up, she takes my wrists and handcuffs me.

"You are under arrest in relation to the death of De-Niece Carmichael. You're not obliged to say or do anything, unless you wish to do so, but whatever you say or do may be used in evidence. Do you understand?"

Nodding my head, dejectedly, I respond, "Yeah, I understand."

Officer Hamilton leads me up the driveway and

places me in the back of the car. When she closes the car door, I start to realise that I'm in some seriously deep shit.

I can't believe this is what my life has become.

When we arrive at the station: I'm fingerprinted, photographed, and placed into a room to be formally interviewed. Sitting in the room, I look around and it hits me again that I took someone's life. I make it to the bin in the corner just before I throw up, again.

Wiping my mouth with my handcuffed hands, I turn around to sit back down, just as Officer Hamilton and another officer enter.

Officer Hamilton offers to get me a glass of water, while the other officer waits, sitting down. I notice him eyeing me suspiciously before looking back at the papers in front of me. She returns with my glass of water and hands it to me, before taking a seat next to the other officer.

Eventually, he looks up and I know that I'm in serious trouble; there is no expression on his face at all. I'm scared as to what he is about to tell me. "I'm Officer Ferguson, this conversation will be recorded and handed to Department of Prosecutions. They will decide if you will be formally charged. In your own words, please tell us what happened this morning at the residence of Jordan and Mackenzie McRoberts?"

I'm nodding at what he is saying, it's all so surreal, and I can't quite believe that this is happening. Taking a deep breath, I close my eyes and recount all the events from today. "Umm, Jordan texted me to go over and be with Kenz, as he had to go into Malt Me 'cause of some issue. He hates her being alone at the moment. When I got there, I noticed my girlfriend's car, and when I was walking down the driveway I heard shouting. I raced down the driveway and when I got to the fence, I saw that De-Niece was on top of Kenz and..." Pausing, I have a drink of water before I continue, "I was stunned to see her punching and hitting Kenz. I dropped the food bags and ran towards them. I pulled her off Kenz and she went through the French doors. I didn't really pay attention to her; I was focused on Kenz. She groaned and I ran over to her, to make sure she was okay. I didn't even hear the doors smash, I was focused on Kenz, it wasn't until I heard her whisper 'see you in hell' that I realised she went through the doors. Kenz moaned again; I'll never forget that sound. I quickly called an ambulance as Kenz was in a bad way, and Jordan had told me she was pregnant. While I waited for the ambulance, I held Kenz in my arms and called Jordan. You guys and he got there and now we're here." Snapping my head to Officer Hamilton, I hesitantly ask, "Do you know if Kenz is all right?"

I zone out, thinking of Kenz, *fuck, she is okay?*

I vaguely remember Officer Douche writing notes as I spoke, but I was on autopilot and didn't really take heed of what was happening around me. I'm brought back to reality when Officer Hamilton reaches over and touches my arm.

"Mike, we don't have any information on Mrs. McRoberts at this time." She pauses, I can see that she's worried and that scares me. "From here, we will print up your statement, and once you have signed it, you will be free to go. The Department of Prosecutions will let us know if manslaughter charges will be laid against you. We will be in touch, either way."

"Fuck me," I say out loud. Then I whisper, "I can't fucking believe this." As I rest my head on the table.

Officer Ferguson adds, "Look, from what you have told us and the previous history regarding Mrs. McRoberts, the deceased, and her recently deceased cousin, I highly doubt that you will be charged, but don't hold me to that." He stands. "I'll go get this typed up for you to sign, and then we will take you home."

"Thanks."

He leaves but Officer Hamilton stays. She looks over at me. "Are you sure you're okay, Mike?"

"Honestly, I have no idea. I killed someone, who turns out wasn't whom I thought they were, and now there's a chance I'm going to jail for it."

"Mike, I agree with Ferguson, I highly doubt you will be charged. Just think of the positive, Kenzie is safe because you saved her."

"We don't know she's safe, no one can tell me and that's killing me."

"Mike, listen to me. She was alive when she left in the ambulance, and that's because of you. You, Mike. Regardless, that you didn't know who Ms. Carmichael was, you saved someone today."

"I guess so, but how do I live with the fact that A: I killed someone. And B: my girlfriend was a fucking psycho bitch, working with the enemy, and C: I fucking killed someone." Pausing, I rest my head on the table. "How the fuck, did I not know?" Slamming my fist on the table, I lift my head up, shaking it from side to side. "How did I now know? I feel like such a chump."

"Don't beat yourself up, Mike. From what I know of these two cases, no one knew."

Officer Ferguson walks back in. "Mike, please read over your statement, and if you agree with it, sign at the bottom. Then you are free to go. But I do need to remind you, that you are not to leave the state or country until the matter is finalised."

Nodding in agreement I take the statement from him and read it over. It's exactly what I said, so I grab the pen, sign at the bottom where is marked, and hand it back to him. "So what happens now?"

"Thanks, the Department of Prosecutions will be in touch to let you know what's going to happen. So as of now, you are free to go, Mike."

"Mmhmm." I manage to say as he undoes my cuffs. I'm lead out of the interview room and escorted to the car park, where Officer Hamilton drives me back to my place.

The car trip is silent but not awkward. There are so many scenarios going through my mind at the moment, I don't know up from down. I'm broken and lost. When we get back to my place, I thank her for dropping me home and then I head inside.

As I'm unlocking the front door, I realise that my car is at Jordan's place. *Fuuuuck*, I think to myself. Once the door opens, I make a beeline for the kitchen and I grab a bottle of tequila from the kitchen. Jose and I sit on the couch together. I plan to get rip-roaring drunk, but first, I text Jordan for an update.

Mike – *Hope all is OK with Kenz and the munchkins*
Jordan – *Yep, all good, asshat. I'm on my way over. Be there in 10*

Ten minutes later, Jordan walks in the front door, and I've already finished a quarter of the tequila. I'm starting to feel numb, and for the first time today, relaxed but empty. Jordan sits down next to me, concern all over his face. "You okay, dude?" Without looking, he grabs the bottle and takes a swig...I wait for it. "Fuck, tequila, uck."

Laughing, I say, "Yep, I needed it after the afternoon I've had. I've just gotten back to the police station."

"What the fuck, dude?" he says, as he goes to the fridge to get two beers.

Taking another mouthful, I laugh and sigh. "Yep," letting the 'p' pop. "I have officially been charged in relation to the death of De-Niece, and I may or may not be fucking charged with manslaughter. Everything has been sent to prosecutions and they will let me know."

"Fucking hell, Mike, are you shitting me?"

"I shit you not, Jordan." Nodding towards the tequila, I add, "Hence, tequila, straight from the bottle." Raising the bottle, I nod towards him and say, "Bottoms up!" I lift the bottle to my mouth and take a drink; I savor flavour as it hits the back of my throat, warmth coursing through me as I swallow. Looking towards Jordan, I ask, "How are Kenz, Mac, and Cheese?"

"Really, Mac and Cheese?"

"Really, really. Now tell me, are they oaky?"

"Yeah, they're all okay. Kenz is pretty banged up, but

she's tough, just like my lil' munchkins. As soon as she found out about you, she sent me here to make sure you were okay. She's worried, Mike. To be honest, I'm worried about you. Are you all right?"

"Dude, I have no fucking clue how I feel right now. I killed someone, my girlfriend was a fucking psycho working with the fucking enemy, and my family has been put through the ringer in the last seventy-two hours. I feel like a chump, a fucking chump. Seriously, dude, I'm so, so sorry."

"What are you sorry for? If it wasn't for you, who knows what would have happened today? I owe you."

"You're not pissed that I was fucking the enemy?"

"Fuck no! You didn't know, dude, hell, none of us knew. How is that your fault?"

"I just feel bad, how the fuck could I not know she was a fucking fruit loop, related to a fuckwit? I'm never going there again, no girlfriend, no relationship...ever."

"Dude, look at me!" I look towards Jordan, after taking another swig of tequila, "This is in no fucking way your fault. Nobody knew, NOBODY." He emphasises nobody.

Putting my hand up, I try to interrupt him, but he ignores me, *asshole.* "We were all clueless when to came to fuckface douche canoe and bitch face mole. This is no one's fault but theirs, Mike. You saved Kenz today, and for that I will be forever in your debt."

I have nothing to say because I don't feel any of that, right at this minute; I doubt I will ever feel any of that. In order to throw him off track, I do the only thing I can, I raise the tequila bottle, before taking another mouthful.

"Dude, my car is still at your place. Can you swing by tomorrow so I can get it?"

"Sure, we can go see Kenz, too. She's really worried about you. Fingers crossed she can come home too, and then we can hang at our place, just like old times."

"Sounds like a plan. Again, I'm so sorry, Jor."

"Stop apologising, Mike, you have nothing to me sorry about."

Jordan and I chat for a while, and I continue to drink my bottle of tequila, but really I just want to be alone. He must sense I want to be alone as he says, "Dude, get a good night's sleep and I'll be back in the morning."

"Yes, Dad." I say like a smart-ass. "Thanks for coming over, it means a lot."

"Anytime, Son, anytime," he says, slapping my leg in a dad-like way.

Standing up, I sway as I'm on my way to pissdom and escort Jordan out. He does the manly one arm hug, back slap, and it feels just like old times, but things will never be the same again; not for me anyway.

After he leaves, I head back inside and shut the front door, sitting back down on the sofa. I finish the bottle of tequila before passing out.

SITTING, ALONE IN THE LOUNGE ROOM, I SADLY LOOK around. I used to love being in this room. It was full of happy memories; Dad sitting in his brown leather recliner, reading, Mum sitting on the caramel sofa, doing her Sudoku puzzles, and Jace and me, sitting on the floor by the bay window playing a game. We were your typical Aussie family but that all changed, in an instant.

Now, this room feels empty, void of any emotions except fear, sadness, and loathing.

Uncle Kelvin comes barging in, shouting, "Where is it? It's mine!" He's drunk, again and his short muscular body sways from side to side as he moves from room to room, searching for something he believes is his. He makes me stay where I am until he has finished searching; not that I want to follow him. I've no idea what he's looking for. Just like every night, when he doesn't find whatever it is, he storms out of here in a mood, slamming the front door behind him.

I cringe when I hear him start his car; he's in no state

to drive with the amount of alcohol coursing through him. As soon as I hear his car back out of the driveway and drive off, I race to the front door and lock it, sliding down until I hit the floor, I cry, the tears pouring out like Niagara Falls.

This has been my life for the past six weeks; and will be for the foreseeable future.

The following night is the same; Uncle Kelvin barges in, searches, and as usual, comes up empty-handed. If only he'd tell me what he's looking for, I could then help him find it, then he would leave me alone and I could get on with my life.

Tonight is a particularly tough night; it would have been Mum's birthday, which was always such a happy occasion. Dad used to spoil her on her birthday every year, thinking about them makes me smile. Then the reality of them being gone hits me and I get upset.

From the library I hear him thrashing around and I start to cry. My eyes well with tears and I'm consumed by grief. Why did he have to come tonight of all nights?

I cry for them.

I cry for me.

I cry for what Uncle Kelvin has become.

I cry for what will never be.

They would be so disappointed right now. Not at me, but at Uncle Kelvin, how could he do this to me? To us? To their memory? We are meant to be family, family doesn't do this to each other.

All this shit started after the reading of the will, everything was left to me, everything: the house, the money, the business, and every single Blac property.

Uncle Kelvin was pissed, beyond pissed, he could not comprehend how his sister wouldn't leave him anything. I would gladly hand everything to him, if it meant that they would still be alive. The only thing stopping me is Mum and Dad's final wishes, I want to uphold their memory as best as I can and make them proud.

Every night I ask what he is looking for, so I can help find it and get rid of him, and every night he won't tell me. He just tells me I'm spiteful like them and I'd lie about it.

I wish I knew what he was looking for.

Pulling my knees closer to my chest, I sit on the sofa in Mum's spot, rocking back and forth, hoping and praying he will leave soon. Hearing something smash, I realise that I need to get out of here. This isn't what Mum and Dad would want for me.

Once again, Uncle Kelvin has stormed out of here, empty-handed. It's so hard, I wish they were here, I miss them everyday, it's getting harder and harder to go on.

Laughing to myself, I thought the hardest thing I have ever done was burying my parents and brother; that was nothing compared to reading the letter they left.

———

...Seven weeks earlier

After leaving the lawyer's office, I came straight home; I flew up the stairs and ran into Mum and Dad's bedroom. I could still smell them, and as soon as their scent hits my nose, the tears started flowing; tears and snot pouring down my face, my body shuddering from the sobs. Jumping onto their bed, I snuggled into their pillows and I cried. Once I had calmed down, I pulled the letter from leather jacket pocket. Holding it in my hands, I stared at Mum's writing for ages before getting the courage to open the beige envelope in my hands.

My eyes welled with tears again, but I gave myself an internal pep talk and finally opened it. Taking a deep breath, I read the final message from my parents. I guess they didn't expect one of us to die alongside them, as the letter is addressed to both, Jace and me; this caused the tears to start again. Finally composing myself, I took a deep breath I read the letter.

To our dearest children, Jace and Savannah,

If you are reading this, then both your father and I are no longer with you. For that I apologise, but please know we love you so very much and we are very proud of you both.

The lawyer would have explained that we have left everything to you both. You will be comfortable for the rest of your lives, you know how to run the company, so we know it will be left in good hands. Knowing that you will be looked after will give both your father and me comfort.

There is a safe in the library with the stocks, some extra cash, and my jewelry. Savannah, the jewelry is yours, please do not let anyone else in the family take this. They can have anything else in the house, but the jewelry is yours and yours only. The code for the safe is your birth date and time; please keep this code and the safe hidden.

There is also a safe deposit box at the bank. Please keep this safe; it is imperative that this remains protected. Do not let anyone know about this. Its contents are extremely important to your father and me, as well as, your grandparents. Please, please, keep this safe and secure; at all costs.

We hope you live full and happy lives. Tell any future grand-children that even though we have never met them, we love them very much. If you are ever lonely or afraid, look up into the sky, and we will be looking down on you, giving you the strength to carry on.

With all our love,

Mum and Dad XoXoX

Lying in their bed, I read the letter over and over. It was after reading it for the third time that I decided to take action. With their words, they gave me the encouragement I needed; even from the grave they were still looking over this. It was that night, I decided to plan my escape from this living hell.

3

KELVIN

WHAT THE EVER-LOVING FUCK? MY BITCH OF A sister and her wanker husband didn't leave me anything, not a fucking cent. They left everything to her, Savannah. "What do you mean I get nothing?"

"I'm sorry, Kelvin, everything has been left to Savannah, and in most cases, that's what happens. Any living descendants inherit directly from their parents."

"Well, this is bullshit!" I shout. Shoving my chair back, I storm out of the lawyer's office, slamming the door behind me. Leaving the solicitor shocked and open-mouthed, and Savannah crying; like the sissy ass bitch that she is. Hearing him console her only makes me even more pissed off. She is now the sole owner of Blac Family Jewelers, and once again, I'm shafted.

Making my way to the Grand, I take a seat at the bar and order a beer and double bourbon. Slamming back the bourbon, the burn on the way down feels good, but I'm still pissed off. Ordering another two shots, I down them one after the other, and now that I'm a little pissy the anger is subsiding.

I can't fucking believe that they didn't leave me anything; it feels just like when Ma and Pa died and they left everything to my sister. Granted she was fifteen years older then me when they passed, and I was still in high school but still, I'm their son. As always, Kelvin misses out and this time, I didn't even get a mention, that's what pisses me off the most. Even from the grave my sister is still messing with me.

Guess now I will just have to have some fun with my dear old niece. She's a push over, so I should be able to find what's mine. It will be just like in high school. She was a few years below me, and with the aid of the basketball team, we used to pick on her. That was until Jace finally hit puberty, man, did he give me as ass-kicking that day...but that lil' fucker ain't here now to protect her. Oh, this is going to be fun.

4

MIKE

It's been four weeks since I took another person's life.

It's been four weeks of torture.

It's been four weeks of replaying that moment over and over.

It's been four weeks of hell.

I'm so lost.

Whenever I close my eyes, I see the same thing: De-Niece on top of Kenz, pulling her arm back, unleashing her fury, and saying the nastiest of things. I'm slowly getting better, I think. I no longer throw up when the memories return, so that's a win...I guess. I've had the same dream each and every night for the past four weeks, and each night I wake up in a cold sweat.

It constantly haunts me that my girlfriend, the person I loved with all my heart, the person who I was just about to propose to, did this to my family. How did I not know she was a psychopath working with a psychopath? Related to a psychopath?

I don't trust anyone anymore; well except for Kenz and Jordan.

One thing I do know, I will never, ever, have another girlfriend. Women only lead to heartache and pain. Random pussy yes, but never a girlfriend.

What hurts the most is that I now hate being around Kenz and Jordan, I let them down. I feel like I should have known. I should have done more. Were the signs there and I missed them? Or am I just weak and stupid? I've gone over our relationship so many times, and I can't believe I didn't know. Seriously, how do you not know your girlfriend is a fucking psycho bitch? I don't know anything anymore.

The silver lining to all of this, I now have a great friend, Officer Hamilton. She and I have struck up a surprising friendship. She is the best wingman ever, she shits all over Jordan. She hates that I always refer to her as Officer Hamilton, but it's too weird calling her Kelly.

———

Tequila is another newly acquainted friend and my way of coping with the dreams. Drinking myself into a stupor so my mind and body are numb, it works most nights, but there is nothing to erase those memories; they will haunt me for all eternity.

A new pub, The Black Dungeon, has just opened up near my house, so I can drink and stagger home. I don't have to worry about driving. I am responsible and shit like that...occasionally.

It's a pretty awesome pub that I hope to bring Jordan

to for a friendly drink, one of these days, if I can get over the guilt and stand to be around him. It's soooo hard to be near him and Kenz; I imagine it would be a lot worse had it been Kenz to die, but thank fuck that didn't happen.

To combat the loss of Jordan, I have a new nonjudgmental non-back chatting bestie: Jose Curevo. Jose and I have become the bestest of friends. He's awesome and best of all, he makes me forget, and forgetting is good.

Another new hobby I've discovered is pussy, random pussy. I fucking love losing myself balls deep inside someone for a few hours. No talking just fucking, it's an awesome way to forget.

My life has become a rotation of booze and pussy, sometimes both at the same time. Being sober makes me remember that girlfriends are nothing but trouble, but pussy is fun.

———

The other night, to mix things up, I decided head into town rather than going to the Dungeon. Walking from bar to bar, I eventually ended up at Club Deux, where I met up with this hot redhead and her blonde friend. What I thought was going to be a quiet night with Jose turned into a night that I will not ever forget.

Don't ask me their names, I have no fucking idea, and to be honest, I don't fucking care. What I can tell you, though, is that I had the most erotic threesome that I have ever had the pleasure to be a part of. There was no judgment or anger, just primal, hot, out of this world fucking. Now I've ventured into threesome territory before, and

I'm definitely a fan, but this night is one that I will go down in the history books.

It all started when Red caught my eye as I walked into the club, my cock immediately twitching when she smiled at me. Her hazel eyes were full of lust, and she was eye-fucking me as I sauntered over to her. Just as I sat down, her blonde friend appeared on the other side of me. Making me the meat in the center of a pussy sandwich, my cock was rock hard and we hadn't even spoken a word yet.

After ordering us a round of drinks, which included several shots, a beer for me and some fruity shit for them, we made small talk. Red threw her drink back before grabbing my hand and leading us to the dance floor. She proceeded to bump and grind her pussy all over me. My hands roamed all around her hot little body. My cock was starting to ache at this point, it was as hard as steel.

Pulling her closer, I sank my tongue into her mouth; she tasted like pineapple. Our mouths moved steadily to the beat of the music while our tongues danced together. Grabbing my hand, she placed it at the apex of her thighs, nudging her dress up, giving me access to her crotch.

Stretching my fingers higher, I discovered she wasn't wearing any undies. In the middle of the dance floor, I rubbed her bare, naked pussy, which was extremely wet from her arousal. Reaching up further, I cupped her pussy and rubbed my palm down her slit; she ground herself against me, moaning into my mouth as she pulled me closer to her body.

Ever so slowly, I ran my finger up and down her slit before plunging inside her tight warm passage, and slipping another finger inside her. I finger-fucked her on the dance floor, while our tongues continued to wrestle for supremacy. She came gloriously over my fingers, throwing her head back and moaning, the entire dance floor oblivious to what we were doing.

Once her orgasm had finished, she pulled my hand out from between her legs and proceeded to suck all her juices off my fingers, while staring deeply into my eyes; holy fucking hotness.

We were about the leave the dance floor when Blondie joined us; she grabbed Red's cheeks and shoved her tongue into her mouth before whispering something. Red looked over at me, smiled seductively before leaning over and kissing me. She tasted like pussy, pineapple, and sex. Breaking our kiss, she winked at me, before turning back towards the bar, leaving Blondie and me alone together in the middle of the dance floor.

Blondie leaned towards me, wrapped her arms around my neck, and smashed her lips against mine, I could taste Red and tequila on her lips as she pulled me closer to her tight sexy body; I groaned into her mouth as our kiss deepened. She started running her hands all over my chest and back, before wrapping her leg around mine and grinding herself on me.

I was lost in our kiss when all of a sudden; I felt a hand reaching around us and it started to grope my cock through my jeans. Opening my eyes, I saw Red behind Blondie, rubbing her pussy on Blondie's ass and nibbling on her earlobe.

My cock got even harder at the sight before me. Reaching over I pulled Red closer to us and shoved my tongue into her mouth, again tasting tequila. Pulling away, I turned my attention back to Blondie, kissing her deeply while gripping Red's ass, squishing Blondie between us.

While I was kissing Blondie, Red leaned over, nibbled on my ear, and whispered, "Let's get out of here." *You don't have to ask me twice*, I thought to myself as I grabbed both of their hands and tugged them towards to bar. Before leaving, we did another round of tequila shots and then headed back to my place.

There was a cab waiting out front, so we all jumped in, again I'm sandwiched between them both. Giving the cabbie my address, I sat back and got comfy as the girls began rubbing my cock, while I alternated between kissing them.

Reaching up, I started to massage Blondie's tits through the thin fabric of her little black dress. From the corner of my eye, I saw her hand slip below the hem of her dress, her legs inching open, inviting me in. Snaking my hand down her tight stomach, I slid my hand under her dress and joined my fingers with hers. Gently parting her pussy lips, we slipped our entwined fingers in an out of her warm wet pussy. She started riding our fingers, when Red's fingers joined us. The three of us finger-fucked Blondie while the two of them rubbed my cock; closing my eyes, I leaned back and enjoyed the ride.

I'm bought back to reality when I heard the cabbie clear his throat, "Umm, we're here." Opening me eyes, I realised that we'd arrived at my place. Looking at him through the rearview mirror, I smirked and threw the fare at him. We exited the cab and headed inside for a night of unforgettable pleasure.

Unlocking the door, we headed inside. Being a gentleman, I offered them a drink; they saw the tequila on the counter from before I went out and wiggled their eyes towards it. I poured three shots and we toasted, and I said, "Bottoms up!" and they giggled.

Red said, "Cheers!"

Blondie looked at me and seductively said, "Here's to a night we will never forget." Watching her do that shot was sexy as hell, my cock started throbbing, and I knew tonight was going to be sexually wild. We had a few more shots before the fun began.

I'd just placed the tequila bottle on the bench when Red grabbed my hand, pulling me into the lounge room. Spinning me around, she pushed me down onto my couch; straddled my lap and attacked my face. Our lips crashed together as she started to ride me, grinding herself over my hardening cock. My cock was ready to explode, it was stiff as a board; I could cut steel with it, it was becoming painful, straining behind my pants.

Blondie must have had a sixth sense because she ran her hands up Red's back, pulling her off me. Together they poured tequila into each other's mouth before kissing each other. The sight before me was so sexual; I'd never been that turned on in my life.

They each climbed onto the couch, on either side of me. Leaning over me, Red poured tequila into Blondie's mouth, who bent down and kissed me, transferring the tequila into my mouth before leaning up and kissing Red deeply. Blondie took the bottle from Red and did the same thing. *Now this is the way to drink tequila*, I thought to myself and smiled, as I felt the burn of the liquid sliding down my throat.

Turning around, she placed the bottle on the coffee table, lowered to her knees and popped open the button on my jeans, unzipping my pants with her teeth. Reaching her hand inside my boxer briefs, she cupped my throbbing cock and lightly squeezed. Lifting up slightly, she edged my pants and boxer briefs down, and finally my aching cock sprang free. Gasping at the size of my cock, she wrapped her tiny hand around me, and stroked up and down.

Red got down onto her knees and the two of them kissed over the tip of my cock, giving me a double head job. Kissing and sucking over the head of my cock, I moaned. Having two mouths on my cock was the best feeling ever, their tongues flicking out, fighting each other for control over my cock.

One of them took my cock into her mouth and sucked while the other stoked and sucked my balls before they kissed each other over the head once again, repeating the process over and over. That was the hottest head job I have ever had. It wasn't long before I exploded, without warning. My milky cum spurted free, their tongues fighting to get a taste.

When I finally came back to earth after my shattering climax, I noticed that they are both naked. Red pushed Blondie back onto the couch, and spread her legs while she dove in; nipping, licking, and sucking her dripping wet pussy.

Grabbing a franga from the coffee table drawer, I

sheathed my cock and knelt behind Red; spreading her ass cheeks before slamming myself balls deep inside her. Her pussy felt like heaven, her moans increased when she screamed, "Fuck me harder!" I picked up the pace and continue to slam in and out of her.

Before either of us came, she crawled up Blondie so their pussies were now rubbing each other. Pulling out of Red, I started to rub my cock up and down Blondie's pussy, plunging deep inside of her. She moaned in pleasure as I slid in and out of her tight passage.

Blondie arched her back and I felt her pussy muscles tighten around my cock. It was enough to push me over the edge, together our orgasms ripped through our bodies.

Red kissed her way up Blondie's chest, her tongue slamming into her mouth; the sight in front of me mesmerized me. Reaching up, Blondie grabbed my hand and together we finger-fucked Red. Our fingers sliding in and out, her breaths became shallow; I knew she was close. Slipping my fingers out of her pussy, I inched around and slipped a finger into her ass. That sent her skyrocketing and she screamed, "Fuuuuck!" Riding Blondie's fingers in her pussy and my finger in her ass, she tumbled over the edge into the abyss of unadulterated pleasure.

The three of us lay here on the couch, catching out breaths as our bodies returned from heaven.

For the rest of the night, we proceeded to fuck in every position possible –*Mr. Kama Sutra would be proud*– and in every possible combination: the three of us together, just Red and I, Red and Blondie sixty-nining each other while I watched, me fucking Blondie while

Red fingered herself watching, Blondie sucking and fingering Red whilst Red deep throated my cock, tweaking her and Red's nipples before reaching a hand down to massage her clit as I spilled down her throat.

It was unbelievably fucking hot, but without a doubt, there was no greater pleasure than having someone ride your pulsating dick while another's bare, slick pussy rode your face, and they tongue wrestled together above you, massaging each others breasts and rubbing their own swollen clits. Nirvana came to mind as I released my load once again.

The crème-del-a-crème of the evening, the final double head job of the night from the Bobbsey twins, but this time I tongue fucked one and finger-fucked the other. I was drowning in pussy pleasure; I could have died in this position, and I would have been a very happy man.

Just before dawn they both get dressed and went home. I was left, lying on the lounge room floor, with the biggest smile on my face.

Best. Night. Ever.

5

SAV

A WEEK AFTER WHAT WOULD HAVE BEEN MUM'S birthday, I started to relax; I was feeling like me again. The stores were doing well and I hadn't seen Uncle Kelvin in a few days. *Maybe he has given up on his quest*, I thought to myself that night when I was in the shower.

After my shower, I climbed into my bed but I couldn't sleep. I lay there staring at the ceiling, a million different scenarios through my head. *What the fuck am I going to do?*

Just before 9:00 p.m. there is a knock at the front door. I sit bolt upright in bed when the knock comes again. Getting up, I walk down the stairs and yell, "Coming!" All of a sudden, a feeling of dread washes over me and I slow my pace.

Reaching the foyer, I swing the door open without checking the peephole; my heart stops, my breathing stills. Standing on the other side of the door is a man in a ski mask. He comes barging in, shoving me into the wall while three other masked men push past into the house.

He tightly wraps his hand around my throat, growling, "Where is it, bitch?"

"Where's what?" I manage to squeak out, the pressure on my throat becoming unbearable.

Just as the stars start to appear in my vision, another masked man comes through the door, shoving the person holding me and snarls, "Enough, we need her coherent."

It's a woman, I think to myself as I clutch my neck and slide down the wall, gasping for breath, tears pouring down my face. The first guy steps away from me and the bitch crouches down. "Sorry for my colleagues, they have no manners when it comes to a pretty girl. Now, tell me where it is."

Through my tears, I manage to say, "Where's what?"

She laughs and slaps my face. "You want to play games, little dove, fine by me but know this, I always get what I want." Standing up, she turns and says, "Search the place, intel says it's here somewhere."

Bending back down to eye level she threatens, "Things will be much easier, little dove, if you just tell me where it is. Simply tell me and we leave."

"I...I...don't know what you are after, tell me what it is, and if I know, I'll tell you, I promise."

WHACK

WHACK

WHACK

"Do I look stupid to you?"

WHACK

"You know what I'm after."

WHACK

"Now tell me and I'll leave you to get back to your measly little life, unharmed."

WHACK

"Lie to me, and I cannot guarantee your safety."

WHACK

Standing up, she leans against the front door, starting intently at me. "I'm waiting," she spits.

"Honestly, I have no idea what you are talking about or what you are looking for."

"Tsk tsk tsk, I don't like liars, Ms. Blac." Stalking towards me, she bends down and grabs me by my shoulders, slapping me hard across the face. Roughly grabbing my upper arms, she shoves me up and marches us into the library.

Looking around, I see majority of the books have been pulled off the shelves. I'm shoved onto the couch and the guy who pushed me against the wall straddles my waist, my heart drops as I think he's going to rape me. He grabs my face, leans down and snarls, "Last chance, bitch, tell us. Where is it?"

The tears are now pouring down my cheeks, taking a deep breath and in a soft voice I stutter, "I...I...I don't know, I don't know." I take a deep breath. "Please just let me go. Please. Please. Please."

He jumps off me and cackles, "He said you were a sooky bitch who'd play dumb. I guess for once a client was right." Shaking his head he walks around the library. "Last chance, bitch, where is it?"

All of a sudden, I get this rush of adrenaline. I stand up, glare at them, and growl through clenched teeth, "I have no fucking idea what you are after, now get the fuck out of my house."

This pisses them off; they look at each other and the lady nods at him. Before I know it, I'm on my back and he is punching and slapping me. "You have a death wish, little grasshopper, tell me where it is and all this will stop." He keeps punching and hitting me. Standing up, he starts kicking me. I can hear them talking, but everything is going fuzzy and it's getting harder and harder to breathe. "The bastard is not gonna be happy." Is the last thing I hear before it all goes black.

———

When I come to, I'm not sure where I am and I start to panic. Blinking a few times to bring my vision back to normal, I look around and realise that I'm in a hospital bed, thankfully I'm alone. Tears well in my eyes and I start to cough. Taking a breath, I wince in pain, it hurts like a bitch. My whole body is aching. Everything hurts.

The door to my room opens and a nurse enters. "Hi, sweetie. I'm Doreen. Do you know where you are?"

"I'm...I'm in hospital." Pausing, I ask, "What happened?"

"You were badly beaten and unconscious when you were brought in. You're a bit banged up, but you are in safe hands now."

"Who...how did I get here?"

"Kelvin, I believe he's your uncle, bought you here."

As soon as she mentions Uncle Kelvin, I start to

panic. My heart rate increases, it becomes hard to breathe. I can hear waves whooshing in my head, mixed with the beeping sound of the monitors in my room going off.

Doreen gently rubs my arms, and in a soothing voice tells me to breathe and calm down; it reminds me of Mum and I start to hyperventilate again. *I miss my mum.* I'm struggling to breathe now, the pain increasing, the panic coursing through my veins in overdrive. Doreen reaches over and pushes a button on the wall behind me. Within minutes, the room is filled with people. Even though I'm in the room; I can't hear or process what they are saying, everything is muffled.

My breaths are now coming in short, fast bursts; it's excruciatingly hard to breathe right now. I'm starting to see black spots; I'm in a full-blown panic attack right now.

All of a sudden, I feel calm, a wave of warmness rushes around my body. I hear Doreen say, "Shhhh, Savannah, let it relax you." She soothingly rubs the hair along my hairline when I start to feel my body relaxing as the sedative makes its way through my system. My breathing evens out, and I start to feel calm, my eyes are heavy and I fall into darkness.

When I wake again a few hours later, Uncle Kelvin is sitting at the end of my bed. Quickly I close my eyes again, I don't want to face him. "I know you're awake," he sneers.

Taking a deep breath, I open my eyes and stare at the window. Before we get a chance to say anything to each other, the nurse comes in. "You're awake, honey, how do you feel?"

Glaring at Uncle Kelvin, I say, "I feel like I've been beaten within an inch of my life and I have no idea why."

"Stop it, child, you're over reacting, as usual," Uncle Kelvin says.

"Excuse me, sir, if you speak to my patient like that again I will ask you to leave. I don't care that you are family."

I whisper to myself, "He's not my family."

Doreen turns back to me and finishes my obs. She smiles at me and I'm pretty sure she heard what I whispered. "Honey, do you remember what happened?"

"It's all pretty fuzzy right now."

"That's understandable, honey. You were unconscious when your uncle bought you in, you were badly beaten." Looking over her shoulder towards Uncle Kelvin she says, "The police want to speak to you when you have a moment." Looking back at me she adds, "Let me know when you are up to it, and I'll arrange it for you."

Uncle Kelvin jumps up. "You need to have an attorney present when you speak to them. You can't trust them."

I lean up on my elbows, the pain radiates through my body, but I stare directly at him and between clenched teeth I growl, "Get the fuck out of my room. I will talk to whom ever I want, when I want. You have no control over me."

Laughing, he shakes his head as he moves to the door, with his hand on the door handle; he looks back at me. "I should've fucking left you there to die...alone." Turning, he opens the door and slams it shut on his way out.

Before the door has slammed, the tears are pouring

down my face, crying hurts but I can't help it. The chasm has opened and there is no stopping the tears. Doreen stops what she is doing and envelops me in a hug. It reminds me of a mum hug and that just makes the tears come quicker. Eventually, I calm down and compose myself, Doreen pulls back, and she looks caringly at me. "Are you okay, honey?"

Shaking my head from side to side, I chuckle; I have no fucking clue about anything now. "I've no idea how I feel right now. All I know is that I hurt all over." My eyes well with tears, I quietly murmur, "I miss my family. I'm all alone." I start to cry again, and again, Doreen wraps her arms around me until I'm all cried out and have calmed down.

I'm kept in hospital for five days, when I'm finally released I'm happy and sad: happy to be out, sad to be going home to an empty quiet house. The first few days at home were tough, I ached from head to toe, and it hurt like a bitch to move. My store manager, Sierra, popped by daily to check on me. Bringing me coffee and cakes most days, just like when I'm at the store with her. I'm so lucky to have great staff to assist me. I've been a bit aloof since I lost Mum and Dad but Sierra really has made things much easier. She has been my rock since I lost everyone, along with my best friend but he is busy setting up a new venture; I'm so proud of him.

Taking the doctors advice, I rest up and do what the hospital physio recommends. I am soon healed, but the bubbly Sav is gone. All that remains is a shell of my former self.

Thankfully, Uncle Kelvin has stayed away; I haven't

seen him since the day I woke up in the hospital. The police have been by twice to interview me, but I'm not much help. The events of that night are still a blur, but deep down, I know who arranged it.

I'm too scared to tell the truth. I wish I were stronger to tell them what I know, but I'm afraid. Hoping that if I play dumb, it will all go away, and I can get on with my life and figure out what he is after. I'm now determined, more than ever, to find out what he is after and keep it safe from his grubby mitts.

I will do whatever it takes to keep what is rightfully mine and uphold Mum and Dad's wishes...whatever it takes.

6

MIKE

THIS WEEK HAS BEEN PRETTY SHITTY, WELL SHITTIER than usual. You'd think I would be on cloud nine as I have officially been cleared in relation to De-Niece's death. Even though legally I'm not responsible, mentally is another story; the guilt is still eating at me.

After getting home from work on Thursday, I throw together a bag, grab my swag, swing via the bottle-o and stock up on beer and tequila, and I head to my property. It's about fifty minutes out of the city. I have ten spectacular acres, it's my happy place and exactly where I need to be right now.

Whenever I'm feeling like shit, or I just want to get away, I head out for a few days and clear my head. The place was covered in tress when I bought it; I had a small patch cleared so I could easily camp. Recently I had a little self-contained cabin built and got the water, electricity, and plumbing services all sorted.

There was a little shed there when I bought the place so I gave it a little refurb while the builder were there.

Shelving was added for all my tools and shit, and I now have a secure place to leave my quad bike and all the gear.

Just my luck, traffic is really, really shit today, and it takes me nearly two hours to get there. By time I arrive, it's just on dusk and I decide that a night under the stars is called for. Rather than staying in the cabin, I unroll my swag, start a fire, set up my camp chair, and settle in.

Cracking open my first beer, I sit back and stare up at the evening sky. The twilight sky is turning black and is filled with dark, ominous clouds; much like how I feel at the moment. My first beer goes down a treat, and I know that this is just what I needed.

Why did I not do this sooner?

Later that night, when I'm well on my way to pissed-dom, my guilt starts to eat away at me again, and the questions begin floating around.

How could I not know that my girlfriend was a fucking fruit loop?

Why did I think with my dick?

How did I miss the signs?

What could I have done differently?

Why oh why, did I meet a skank named De-Niece Carmichael?

The next morning, I'm woken to the sun glaring in my face, with a stiff neck and sore body from passing out in my chair. After restoking the fire, I take a piss and call work. I tell my boss that I need a personal day today; thankfully she is great and tells me it's okay. Not that I really give a shit, I wasn't coming in no matter what she said.

I'm starting to get hungry, so I get up and head into the cabin; unpacking the food and stuff that I bought from home. Switching on the kettle, I make myself a coffee and cook myself scrambled eggs and bacon for breakky. When I've finished and cleaned up, I grab a shower and decide to spend the morning quad biking. Once I have on my safety gear, I head off. This was just what the doctor ordered. I spend the next few hours cruising around the property and forgetting about all my worries. *Fuck, I love this place*, I think to myself as I watch a family of kangaroos graze on the grass.

Later that morning, my phone starts to play, *Wash it All Away* by Five Finger Death Punch, and I groan. I'm not in the mood to deal with Jordan right now, so I ignore it. Not five minutes later, it rings again. This time I decline the call and send it straight to voicemail. I've never done that to Jordan before. It pretty much rings again straight away. Again, I decline it but this time, I put it on silent as well. I don't want to deal with anyone at the moment. I just need Mike time...beer...Chicken Twisties...and tequila.

After taking a walk around my property, I grab another beer and decide I need some tunes. Getting my Bose mini player from the car, I set it up. Picking up my phone to connect it, I see that I have fifteen missed calls and five texts from Jordan. I start to feel guilty for ignoring him. Shaking my head, I say, "Fuck it." I just can't deal with him, or anyone, at the moment.

Once again, that day keeps playing over and over in my head; I'm just glad it ended the way it did and that I got there in time. There is no fucking way I could live with myself if anything had happened to Kenz...or Mac and Cheese, I decide to numb the pain with more beer and tequila.

Grabbing another beer and my bottle of tequila, I take up residence next to the fire. The afternoon is spent sitting by the fire, drinking beer, shooting tequila, and getting absolutely hammered. I think to myself that a batch of Kenzie's famous brownies would be awesome right about now.

Sexual Healing by Marvin Gaye comes on and I change up the words to Tequila Healing instead, I think it's pretty awesome, so I put the song on repeat.

Get up, get up, get up, get up!
Wake up, wake up, wake up, wake up!
Oh, tequila let's get down tonight
Ooh tequila, I'm hot just like an oven
I need some lovin'
And tequila, I can't hold it much longer
The bottle's getting lower and lower
And when I get that feeling
I want tequila healing
Tequila healing, makes me feel so fine
Helps me to forget that she was a fuckin psycho
Tequila healing, baby, is good for me
Tequila healing is something that's good for me

I'm pretty hammered and that song has been sung quite a few times. I'm feeling pretty good right now, and by good

I mean, numb. The best thing about being hammered, I forget all of my worries and my shitty fucked up life.

Just before midnight, I stoke the fire up, climb into my swag, and stare up at the night sky. There are millions of tiny little stars, twinkling on a midnight black background; it's an amazing how many stars there are out here without the city lights obscuring them. Sighing, I start to wish that I were a million miles away, living a happy carefree life on one of those twinkly little stars.

———

A few days later, just after lunch, I hear a car coming up the driveway. Looking over, I see Jordan's Jeep stirring up dust as he eases to a stop near the shed. *Shit, I'm in trouble as both McRoberts are here.* Kenz is the first to get out and she looks pissed, Jordan is next and he looks just as pissed.

Stalking over to me, Kenz unleashes her wrath. "Mike Mustange, you have had us all worried." Poking me in the chest. "You take off for five days and don't tell anyone where you are going. You ignore Jordan's calls and mine. You have some explaining to do, mister." She's right up in my face at the moment, she's fuming by now. Her hands are on her hips, her big, beautiful, pregnant belly is right at eye level, her eyes are full of fury, but I also see relief in them as she stares at me, waiting for my reply.

"Well, hello to you too, Kenz. I'm fine; thanks for asking." Leaning forward, I place my hands on her belly, and in that weird voice that people use around kids and babies, I say, "And how are my two favourite munchkins?

Giving Mummy grief, I hope." Winking up at Kenz, I say this.

"Not funny, Mike, you've had us all worried. You've been gone for five days, five fucking days, Mike."

"What do you mean five days? I only just got here."

Jordan whacks me up the side of the head. "Dude, it's Monday. You've been MIA since Thursday. I'm guessing by the size of Mount Canmore and Tequilaville over there, that you've drunk yourself into a stupor and the days have all blended into one." Pulling up a chair, he sits next to me. "Mike, dude, talk to us. What's going on? And don't say nothing. You've not been the same since the shit with douche face and De-Niece went down. You're pulling away from us, drinking waaaaay too much; you're not yourself, dude. Kenz and I are worried about you."

"Holy fuck, five days, really? It seriously feels like I only got here yesterday. I'm sorry, guys, I just needed to get away."

Kenz comes back to join us and hands us all a coffee, I didn't even realise that she disappeared. Fuck, I really am off the rails. Taking the coffee from Kenz, I take a sip. "Thanks, Kenz. I'm sorry to have worried you guys. I'm just not in a good place at the moment." Looking over at Kenz, I put my coffee down, taking a deep breath. "I feel guilty, so fucking guilty."

Kenz leans back and rests her hands on her belly. "Why do you feel guilty? What did you do, Mike?"

"I fell in love with a monster and that monster nearly killed you, Mac, and Cheese." I lower my head in defeat.

"Mike Mustange, you look at me and you listen. It

was not your fault that she was a psycho fucking bitch, psycho runs in the family I'm guessing..."

"But..." I interrupt.

"Shut the fuck up, Mike, and let me finish."

"Wow, feisty, Kenz, is in the house."

"Seriously, Mike, you did nothing wrong. None of us knew. None of us." Kenz waves her fingers in a circle between the three of us and emphasises none of us the second time.

"Yeah, but..."

"No, Mike. There are not buts in this scenario. YOU DID NOT FUCKING KNOW. No one did, PLUS if it weren't for you, I wouldn't be here. You saved me and the munchkins, Mike, YOU!" She puts an emphasis on you.

Jordan pipes in. "Dude, she's right, as usual." He blows a kiss to Kenz after saying this. "This is no one's fault, except for Clint and De-Niece. They both paid the price for their actions and that is not on you."

"I know all of this, but how did I not know? That's what I cannot get past. I feel like a chump."

Kenz gets up and squats down in front of me, "Mike, listen, we were all chumps. If anyone is to blame, it's me. I'm the one who let Clint into our lives, but my therapist made me realise that it's not our fault, we cannot control other people's actions. Maybe you need to go and see her, she really is awesome, and I think it will do you the world of good."

"I'll think about it, Kenz." She glares at me. "Fine, text me her number and I'll give her a call." Looking over at Jordan, I add, "Dude, is she hot?"

We all laugh, Kenz says through giggles, "I think

you'll be just fine, Mike." Kenz smiles and winks at me. She tries to get up but with her big, pregnant belly she is kind of stuck. I can see her mind ticking over as to how she's going to get up.

"Need a hand there, fatso?"

Glaring at me she snarls, "Did you just call me fat?"

"Yep, now do you want a hand? Or do you want to squat there all day?"

"Just help me up, asshole."

Laughing, I get up and help Kenz stand. I wrap my arms around her and pull her in for a big squeezy hug. She wraps her arms around me tightly; we stay that way for a few moments. Pulling back, she smiles at me, and for the first time since it all happened, I think that I will be okay. "Thanks, Kenz. I really appreciate your kind words, even if I don't agree with them."

The three of us spend the rest of the day sitting by the fire, catching up, just like old times, it felt amazing to be Mike again. Just before dark, Kenz and I load a shit-faced Jordan into the Jeep. He's had a few too many beers and is gibbering about loving us both so much, and how he cannot wait to be a daddy. This makes both Kenz and I smile; drunk Jordan is fun relaxed doesn't-have-a-care-in-the-world Jordan, non-drunk Jordan is serious and straight laced and great to be around, but not as entertaining as drunk Jordan. Kenz gets into the driver's seat and winds down the window. "Are you sure you'll be okay, Mike?"

"Yeah, Kenz, I will. I just needed to get away, clear the noggin. I promise I'll head back to reality tomorrow."

"Glad to hear it. Why don't you come over for dinner?"

"Sounds good, Kenz. Thank you. You know I love you, right?"

"Yeah, I do and I love you, too, Mike. See you tomorrow at our place for dinner, that way I know you will be home and safe."

"Night, Kenz. Promise to be there for dinner." Standing there, I wave and watch her drive off, not quite believing that I will be okay, but I do know that I need to change how I'm living my life. I want to be me again.

After waving them off, I grab another beer, a packet of Chicken Twisties and sit by the fire to once again drown my sorrows. My last thought, before I pass out, is that my life will never be the same...never.

7

SAV

It's a sunny Tuesday afternoon, three weeks after being released from hospital; I'm sitting in the library with a cup of coffee, reading *Fractured Affections* by Elizabeth Wills on my iPad. It's a heartbreakingly beautiful story, and I have a total crush on the lead dude. I'm currently hoping someone like him will come to life and rescue me from this living hell. As I'm gazing out the window towards the garden, I realise that I haven't seen Uncle Kelvin for over a week now. It makes me smile and I start to relax; maybe this is all over.

Later that afternoon, I grab a glass of wine and head back to the library, which has become my new favourite room. Snuggling down on the brown suede lounge, I stare into the fire. The cracking of the burning timber and the flickering flames relaxing me, there is nothing more soothing than a glass of wine while sitting by the fire. Gazing into the fire, I realise that I'm smiling and finally, I feel like me again, and dare I say it, happy.

No sooner had I finished that thought and Uncle

Kelvin comes barging through the front door. *I really need to get the locks changed,* I think to myself. Tonight, he can hardly stand up; he's pissed as a fart. The smell of whisky permeates the air and I can smell it from where I'm sitting. *This isn't going to be good,* I think, as he stumbles into the room. He doesn't say a thing, the quietness is disturbing. He plonks himself down on Dad's recliner, it creaks under his weight and roughness and I cringe. He glares at me, and sneers, "Where is it, you little bitch?"

I've had enough of this and tonight I'm feeling brave. "I have no idea what you are looking for, asshole, tell me and maybe, just maybe. I can help you."

"You're just like your mother, a lying vindictive little whore. What she had is just as much mine as it was hers, and now you're hiding it from me."

"I...." but I don't get to finish my sentence as he lunges towards me, slamming his hands on my thighs, the sting of the slap tingling as he gets up in my face and snarls, "Where is it, bitch?"

My heart is racing, my happy feeling of moments ago evaporating, being replaced by unyielding fear. I stutter, "I...I honestly don't know what you are looking for."

He raises is left hand and it collides with my cheek, it stings like a bitch. "Fucking little liar." He turns around and storms out of the house, slamming the front door behind him with such force that the windows and paintings on the walls rattle.

Pulling my legs up, I hug them and cry. Resting my forehead on my knees, I continue to cry, and before I know it, it's pitch black outside, the only light coming from the fire. Standing up, I head upstairs to shower and hopefully wash away the horrible memories of today.

When I'm in the shower, I decide that for my safety and sanity, I need to leave and get away from Uncle Kelvin and any other thugs that he may send after me.

It's time to take my life back, and it starts now.

8

MIKE

My life has become a cycle of going to work, drinking myself stupid, enjoying myself in random pussy, and occasionally sleeping. The guilt still eats away at me, I wish I could turn it off and be me again, but life's a bitch, just like my ex.

It's a bright and sunny Sunday morning, and it's been three weeks since Kenz and Jordan intervention at the property. My head is still all over the place and I still feel like shit. No matter how many times I'm told it's not my fault, I still feel responsible; I really wish I would let it go and be me again.

I was fucking the devil herself, how is one meant to get over that?

I'm in the laundry shoving my sheets into the dryer when I get a text. Digging my phone out of my pocket, I see it's Officer Hamilton.

Officer Hamilton: *Hey Mike! Wanna meet up for a beer?*

Me: *Sounds good. Name the time and place*
Officer Hamilton: *Malt Me at 3pm*
Me: *Sunday arv sesh sounds good to me, c u then*

Not really keen on the location, but the company and beers will be great, I still feel like everyone there gives me the evil eye due to what went down, but maybe it's all in my head.

I took Kenzie's advice and I have been seeing her therapist, Jeannie. She is helping, but I think it will be a long road. Maybe facing everyone at Malt Me is what I need to do, rather than hiding away like the pussy I've become. The old Mike would face it head on and that's exactly what I'm going to do. "Bring it, assholes," I say, as I'm getting out of the shower.

I'm getting out of my cab when another pulls up and Officer Hamilton gets out. She sees smiles, waves. "Hey, Mike."

"Hey! Officer Hamilton."

"Seriously, call me Kelly. I'm not on duty."

"Yeah, but it's so cool saying Officer Hamilton. If it makes you feel better, just call me 'Hot Dude.'"

"Yeah, that's not gonna happen, 'Mr. Not Hot Dude.'" She air quotes my non-nickname, "Let's get our drink on."

"Yeah, nah, that name's not gonna happen, Officer Hamilton, but yes, let's get our drink on." Throwing my arm over her shoulders, we walk into Malt Me for an afternoon of beer, fun, and shenanigans.

Being a Sunday arvo, the place is packed, as usual.

Looking around I can't help but smile. I'm so happy for Kenz and Jordan, their dream has come true. They have managed to turn Malt Me into something awesome. After all the shit that went down, they really deserve all the happiness and success in the world. Looking over at Officer Hamilton, I say, "I'm so proud of all that Kenz and Jordan have achieved with this place."

"Yeah, it is pretty amazing. The guys at the station love it here, especially when they have the live band here playing." Pushing me towards the bar, she says, "I'll get us a table, you get the beers. And a serve of wings too, please, I'm starving."

With a mock salute, I say, "Sir, yes, Sir," and I march towards the bar. I'm leaning on the timber bar, when a head pops up and it's Jordan. "Hey, asshat, didn't realise you were working today."

"Amy and Heather both called in sick, so I'm here helping out. It's actually been fun being behind the bar again. I think I need to do it more often. What brings you here today? Got a hot date?"

"Get fucked, no dating for me. Just here with Officer Hamilton for a catch up." I point over my shoulder towards where she is sitting

"You hit that yet?" Jordan says, nodding in head in her direction.

"Nope, and not going to. I don't like her like that. She's just a mate, a good mate. She's the female version of you."

"So she's awesome then?"

"If you say so, asshat." I quickly change the subject

because my love life is and always will be non-existent. "Where's our sexy mumma-to-be?"

"In the office. She wants to get all the paperwork and stuff sorted before Mac and Cheese arrive." He places two beer mugs and a jug of Grid Mesh Larger on the bar for me, I don't even have to ask, he knows exactly what I like.

Smiling, I raise my eyebrows. "Duuuude, you called them Mac and Cheese."

He chuckles, "Yeah, we all are, well except Kenz. Even Dr. Green is calling them Mac and Cheese."

"My work here is done then." Laughing, I grab the beer mugs and jug. "Hey, if you get a break, come join us." Looking around I add, "It's pretty packed today, I'm so happy for you guys."

"Yeah, it is pretty bloody awesome." Pausing, after looking around, he adds, "Dude, I own a fucking brewery. I still find it amazing that my drunken idea at the Oktoberfest has come to fruition."

"Wow, look at you using big words." He gives me the finger. "Okay, I'm off to get my drink on. See you when you pop over."

Walking across the bar, I smile when I realise that she grabbed a table near the glass wall that looks into the brewery; this table has unofficially become mine. She looks up and smiles. "Took your time, I'm dying of thirst here, dude."

"Ohh, poor baby." I place the jug and mugs on the high top and take a seat. She goes to pour us each a beer when she realises that they are already full.

"Shit, I forgot your wings."

Slapping the table she says, "Totally knew you would, so I flagged down a waitress and already ordered some."

Faking hurt, I cross my hands over my heart and look at her with sad, puppy dog eyes. She laughs, shaking her head. "Suck it up, princess," Picking up her beer, she raises it and toasts, "Cheers, to a beertabolous afternoon."

Clinking our glasses, I add, "To a beertabolous afternoon," before taking a sip. "Man that's a good drop, my man Jordan sure knows how to brew wickedly awesome beer."

"He sure does."

Jordan and Kenz join us before they leave. Kenz is huge at the moment and has the cutest little waddle when she walks. I mentioned it to her once and got a tongue-lashing. I didn't mean to offend her, but I guess when it's weight related, chicks will take it the wrong way, no matter how innocent it was meant.

Officer Hamilton and I have a great afternoon and for the first time in weeks, I don't think of what happened, or that it's my fault. But most of all, I don't feel like the staff here is judging me. Maybe things are going to be okay after all.

EVERYTHING IS SET, THIS TIME NEXT WEEK; I'LL BE free. I will leave my home, my friends, my life, and never have to see Uncle Kelvin again...I hope. As much as it bugs me to know what he is looking for, getting away is my only chance for survival and happiness. There is still quite a lot to do before I sneak away, but for the first time since losing everyone, I'm excited for the future.

Tonight, I was given a reprieve; Uncle Kelvin didn't come over. Since I made the decision to leave, he's been here every night, sometimes twice. This is the first night in weeks that he hasn't been by, I take that as a good sign and that me leaving is the right thing to do.

Next on the leaving list is to go to the bank and get the items in the safety deposit box; I'll set up another when I get settled. If the lawyer hadn't mentioned it to me the day of the will reading, I wouldn't have even known about it.

Before heading to the bank, I grab two coffees and I head to the store to meet with Sierra and go over my plan.

She is the only one who knows I'm leaving for good, but she doesn't know why and to be on the safe side, she doesn't know where I am going.

Sierra is all up to date with everything and I have said good-bye to all the staff. They think I'm just getting away for a bit to clear my head, and they all wish me well. We get to the door and I embrace Sierra tightly. "Thank you for everything, Sierra, I would be lost without you."

"It's my pleasure, Savvy. You are like family to me and I'm happy to help." Pausing she whispers, "Your secret is safe with me, I promise not to let anyone know that I know."

Pulling back from our hug, she takes my hand and squeezes it tightly as I walk out the door. Turning around, I wave and head towards the bank.

After going through all the security checks at the bank, I'm led into the safety box deposit room. Taking a deep breath, I unlock the box and open it. As soon as I lift the lid and see what's inside, I know this was what Uncle Kelvin has been looking for.

Taking another deep breath, I remove everything from the box and place it into my backpack. I relock the box; sign the forms to close it, and I quickly get out of here. As I'm walking out, I start to giggle, *You'll never get it now, asshole*, I think to myself with a wickedly happy smile on my face.

Exiting the bank, my eyes keep darting everywhere. I'm scared of running into my uncle, I'm not sure I could lie to him if he asks what I'm doing or what's in the bag. Once I'm outside, I inhale deeply, hold my breath, and quickly make a run for it. Climbing into my car, I sigh and let out the breath that I was holding. Thankfully, I never saw Uncle Kelvin or anyone, I'm sure I had some help from Mum and Dad today. Again I take this as another sign that I am doing the right thing.

Tomorrow is the first day of my new life.

10

KELVIN

It's so frustrating, first the little bitch didn't die with the rest of them, and now she won't tell me where it is. As soon as she hands it over, I will leave her alone...maybe. Her innocent act is starting to grate on my nerves. She's a lot tougher than I gave her credit for, even those goons couldn't find it, or get it out of her. The beating she took was brutal; I'm impressed she didn't cave. *I'm going to have to up my game if I'm to get what is rightfully mine.*

I'm currently at the Grand and not in the mood to deal with her whinging, whiny, woe-is-me crap, so I decide to stay here and get acquainted with Jack. *I might stop by the brothel on my way home,* I think to myself as I throw back another shot of Jack. Having a few days break will be great, I fucking love seeing the look on her face when I barge in.

Today has really dragged on and my last meeting really pissed me off. *A night of terrorising the little bitch will be fun*, I think as I'm driving down the street.

Pulling up at the house, I see a 'For Sale' sign out the front and my blood starts to boil. "What the fuck is she up to now?" I ask out loud, just as I see Cheryl, the real estate agent coming out.

She comes over to my car. "Good evening, Kelvin, I didn't think you'd be by tonight. I was just finalising the listing photos for Savannah. The town won't be the same without her."

"What?" I spit.

"She left town."

"What do you mean she left?"

"She told me it was too much living in the house, so she's decided to sell and leave town."

"What the fuck?"

Cheryl looks shocked at my outburst. "I thought you knew, you are family after all."

"Hmm, yeah, well the little bitch didn't tell me. What did she do with all the stuff?"

"The movers were here today. They left about an hour ago." Cheryl looks at her watch. "I have to run to another appointment, Kelvin. It was nice seeing you again." She waves as she turns and walks to her car.

Standing on the pavement, I look up at the house. As soon as Cheryl is gone, I race up the driveway, head around the back, and use my key to get inside. Maybe with the house empty I will find what I'm after. I put my key in the lock but it won't turn, "Son of a fucking whorebag bitch!" I shout when my key won't budge. I mumble, "The little ho changed the locks on me, I knew she had what I was after. Well, looks like I will just have to hunt the lil' cunt down."

As I walk back to my car, I dial my guy and ask him to find her. She won't get far and when I find her, she's going to pay.

11

MIKE

...Present day

As usual, I'm sitting at the bar at the Dungeon, trying to drown my sorrows and forget about all the shit that has happened and how crappy my life is at the moment. Maybe tomorrow I will wake up and realise that it was all a dream, and I never met De-Niece, and she didn't ruin my life.

From time to time, I go and visit Kenz and Jor but they have it tough at the moment. Kenz delivered Mac and Cheese eight weeks early, and they had to stay in hospital, but today is the day that they get to come home. I don't know how they do it. I'm not as strong as them and I still feel guilty for everything. I know they have said that they don't blame me, and that I need to move on, but it's pretty hard not to feel like a chump.

Sav, the hot new bartender has just placed my beer in front of me when my phone lights up, it's still on silent from being at work. Jordan is calling me, but I'm not in the mood to talk, so I let it go to voicemail. As usual, he doesn't leave a voicemail; he immediately sends a text.

Jordan – *Yo asshat, we just got home with Mac and Cheese, would love to catch up*

For the first time in a few weeks I smile, those two little munchkins have me wrapped around their little chubby fingers. The thought of seeing Mac and Cheese makes me happy.

Looking up, I see Sav staring at me. She quickly looks away, but my smile only gets bigger when I realise that she was checking me out. *No, Mike, don't go there,* I tell myself, as I ask Sav to settle the bill. Looks like I'm going to Jordan and Kenzie's place tonight.

Mike – *Sounds good to me, be there soon*
Jordan – *Great. Can you pick up dinner on your way. Thanks. Your choice*

His reply is totally something that I would do, and I can't help but laugh, garnering a few strange looks from those sitting at the bar nearby. Bringing food is the least that I can do, it's been a rough few weeks for them.

After settling the bill, I finish off my beer, wave bye to Sav and head off to go see my lil' munchkins, ohh and Kenzie and Jordan. As I'm walking to my truck, I let him know I'm on my way.

Mike – *No worries asshat. Chinese and I are on our way*

Kung Fu Palace is the best Chinese place in town, even though it's out of the way, I don't mind. I order way too much food for three people: two lots of spring rolls, three lots of steamed dumplings, large special fried rice, snow pea and cashew chicken, sweet and sour pork, sizzling beef, honey chicken and Mongolian lamb.

While waiting, I head to the bottle-o next door; a celebration is called for because Mac and Cheese finally came home today, so I decide to splurge. I buy a case of GH Mumm and a bottle of Jack Daniels single barrel, so we can finally wet these babies' heads; *I love this tradition.*

Parking my car in my usual spot on the front lawn, I walk in the front door. I no longer knock, but after what I just saw when I walked in, from now on I will knock and wait for the door to be opened. Kenz is sitting on the couch, tits out, which are massive by the way, and she's feeding Mac...or Cheese, not sure which one. "Fuck, Kenz, put those titties away or at least put a sign up on the front door."

"Mike, watch your language and you can knock, that's what polite people do."

"Pfft, A. I'm not polite and B. Not a chance in hell if I get to see those babies every time." I look towards Jordan and give him a nod and wink; Kenzie's tits look amazing all milk filled. I think to myself, *Wonder what her milk tastes like, wonder if she'd let me try it.* Kenz just shakes her head as she does up her top and smiles at me. *Damn keep those babies out for a little longer,* I wish to myself.

Jordan walks over to me to help with the food and drinks. He smacks me up the side of the head before grabbing the Jack Daniels and bubbly. "Mike, I know what you are thinking and no ducking way."

How the fuck does he know what I'm thinking? That's when I realise that I am still staring at Kenz, standing in the doorway. "Come on, dude, you don't know what goes on in my mind."

From the lounge Kenz laughs, "Yeah, not much at all goes on up there." She winks at me like I just did to Jordan.

"Lucky I love you, baby girl." I place the bags on the table and I walk over to Kenz, placing a quick kiss on her forehead. Looking down I see Mac and Cheese are lying on the couch. They have gotten so much bigger since I saw them last. *I really need to come over more often.*

Kenz and Jordan put the kids down while I set up the feast; I totally ordered way too much food. We all sit down to eat, my eyes keep glancing at Kenzie's chest, and each time Jordan kicks me under the table. It feels just like old times, and for the first time when I'm around them, I don't feel guilty or think about De-Niece and all the shit that has happened.

As I'm driving home later that night, I smile and think that maybe life isn't so bad after all and that everything will work out fine.

12

SAV

I'S BEEN JUST OVER SIX MONTHS SINCE I MADE MY escape, and I finally feel content and happy. No longer am I constantly looking over my shoulder in fear that he will have found me, he's not that smart...I hope.

Some days are harder that others but generally speaking it's all good. I miss home, but mostly I miss my friends. I feel bad skipping out like that but I had no choice, I needed a clean getaway. I certainly do not miss my uncle, that's for sure. I so wish that I could have been there to see the look on his face when he got to the house to find it for sale and then to discover that the locks were changed; it would have been priceless.

Sierra called me the day after I left and said that Kelvin came barging in, just as the store was opening. He was fuming that I had taken off and was spewing obsceni-ties; it wasn't until she threatened him with calling the police that he left.

Deciding to sell the house was tough, but I needed a

new start, and I know that Mum and Dad would have
been proud of me for making that decision. Deep down, I
know that they would have been happy that I wasn't
letting my uncle win.

The house sold immediately, which I knew it would,
it's a lovely house. It selling quickly only confirmed that I
had made the right decision; I know that the new family
will love the house as much as we did.

The local store was and still is operating well; thanks
for Sierra and the amazing staff working for us, well me
now, which is a bonus. All the stores are currently doing
well, and in this economic climate, it amazes me. Profits
were through the roof when I left, and from the recent
reports, they are still going up. Sierra and I chat at least
once a month, unless there is an issue that I need to
tend to.

When I went in to tell them that I was leaving, it's
was really difficult. I didn't elaborate as to where, or how
long I'd be gone, but I informed them that Sierra knows
how to reach me if I'm needed. I did stress that I didn't
want Uncle Kelvin to know where I was, and they were
only too happy to oblige. He's not very well liked in town.
I'm so lucky that the staff are happy to look after the store
for me. I trust them, just like Mum and Dad did.

As soon as I arrived, I opened another safety deposit
box and placed everything from Mum and Dad's into this
one. Keeping it safe, just like they wanted.

Things are finally getting back to normal. I left my
old life behind and I'm getting on with my new life,
tending bar at the local tavern, The Black Dungeon,

something completely different for me. Hopefully it will make it harder for my uncle to find me, if he is even looking for me, that is. Working at the Dungeon is great, the staff is fun and the customers are awesome; it makes work exciting. I've become quite close to one of my colleagues, Jodi. She's awesome, loves a wine or five, is obsessed with milk bottle lollies, and has a beautiful soul. We hit it off immediately and are heading out this weekend for a night of dancing and wine, shockingly we are both off on Friday night. I can't wait to let loose. I can't remember the last time I went out and had fun. I'm pretty excited for my night with Jodi.

There's this one guy who comes in all the time, Mike Somethinstang, he is one fine specimen, and I can't stop thinking about him. Closing my eyes, I remember the first time we laid eyes on each other: I was behind the bar and when I stood up, right before me was Mike, my heart skipped a beat, and my undies immediately became wet. His blue eyes were staring back at me, and I became jelly and all giddy. I've never felt like this around a guy before. I'm pretty sure that I made a complete fool of myself in that moment, but it doesn't matter, I don't need anyone in my heart, or life.

He broke our staring contest and ordered a beer with a tequila shooter; a man after my own heart. After I pulled his beer and poured his shot, he turned looked around for somewhere to sit, before turning back to the bar and taking a seat there, my section for the night.

All night long, I kept sneaking glances at him. He's smoking hot, kind of like Jason Statham—six plus foot tall, broad shoulders, and muscular tattooed arms. His crystal blue eyes were boring into me at one point, my cheeks heated with excitement and my undies became wet; again.

There was something intriguing about him and I couldn't help but smile back. My eyes roamed over his face, taking in his chiseled jaw, hidden by a scruffy yet well-groomed goatee. His bald head shining in the overhead light and a smile that lit up when I smiled back at him. And the kicker, he was a beer with a tequila chaser guy; my exact choice of poison.

Over time, I've tried a few times to flirt with him, which is totally against my rules, he flirts back...I think, but it never advances further than flirting. When I got this job, I told myself that I would never date a customer, but I'm really attracted to Mike, and I know he is attracted to me, too.

When we chat, it feels like we are the only two people around, everything around us fades away and it's just us. We are two atoms drawn together, but there is an invisible force holding each of us back. Some days I let my guard down and try to push through the invisible fence, but it's strong and unbreakable. It's probably for the best, since I'm running and trying to protect what's mine.

Some nights, he looks broken, alone, and sad when he comes in. When I see him like this, all I want to do is jump over the bar and wrap him in a hug. Then I'd kiss away his worries, and we'd have hot, dirty, kinky, mind-blowing, out-of-this-world sex on the pool table.

Other nights, he is so happy and carefree, these are

the nights that he flirts up a storm but he never acts upon it. I've casually asked Jodi and the others about him, but none of them know much about him either.

The nights he doesn't come in I feel sad and empty, I can't explain the feelings that he brings out in me. I wish I knew if he felt the same way about me, it would then help me decide if I should take a chance or not. However, if he approached me, I'd say yes before he even gets to finish the sentence.

Lately, I find that when I'm alone, my thoughts immediately wander to him. Whenever I close my eyes, his face pops into my mind and I immediately smile; my heart rate increases and pulsating sensations build between my thighs. This vision is a nightly visitor when alone in bed. At the rate I'm going, I'll need to replace B.O.B. soon, but Mike is totally worth it.

————

It's Friday afternoon and Jodi will be here soon for pre-going out drinks. The tunes are cranked, and I'm adding the finishing touches to my make-up, when there's a knock at the door. I quickly finish putting on my lippy and as I'm walking down the hallway, I yell, "Coming!"

Opening the door, I say, "Hey, Mole." Jodi is standing on my doorstep with a bottle of sambuca in one hand, bubbly in the other, and a huge smile on her face. Her chocolate brown hair has been straightened and her make-up is flawless. As I hug her hello, I add, "Holy smokes, woman, you look hot."

Stepping aside, I let her into my duplex. She places

the bottles on my coffee table and excitedly replies, "I know, right? But Mole, you look hawt. That top makes your eyes pop and holy shit; your ass in those jeans is out of the world hot. Wish my ass looked like that."

"Whatevs, Jodi, I wish I had your legs. They look like they go all the way to heaven." Winking, I say, "Let's get this party started."

"They sure do go to heaven," she says, with a smug look on her face before grabbing the sambuca, taking the cap off, and taking a swig. Shaking my head at her, I laugh and know that we are going to have the best time tonight.

I head to the kitchen to grab two champagne glasses, but when I get back to the lounge room, Jodi is chugging from the bottle. She smirks and shrugs her shoulders when she sees me. We both start laughing as she places the bubbly back on the coffee table.

"I love your place, Sav, it could do with a new paint job, though."

"Yeah, I asked the landlord and he's happy for me to repaint. He's even going to supply the stuff."

"Wow, that's awesome. I'm still waiting for my outside light to be repaired. It shocks me every time I switch it on."

"Holy shit, that sucks." Grabbing the bottle I take a sip and cough, sambuca isn't my drink of choice. "Sorry, not really a sambuca fan, tequila is my poison." Jodi digs into her bag and produces a bottle and hands it to me with a big smile. "You are awesome, woman."

"Again, I know. I couldn't resist seeing you have a

drink before I gave this to you. I remember you saying, one night to a customer drinking tequila, that it was your all-time fav."

Smiling as she says this, because I know the customer whom she is talking about is Mike. "I say a lot of shit to customers, but that was one time I was telling the truth."

Twisting the cap off the bottle, I look to Jodi and say, "Cheers, Mole!" We clink our bottles together and take a drink. I love the warmth that spreads through my body as the tequila slides down my throat. I close my eyes and savor the flavour until I hear Jodi clear her throat. "Fuck me, woman, that was erotic, watching you drink that. You really do love tequila."

Nonchalantly, I just shrug my shoulders, I mean, what am I to say to that? I take another sip and emphaise my enjoyment. We both start laughing as I place the tequila bottle onto the coffee table. "So, where are we doing dinner?"

"Eating is cheating, Sav."

"I need to eat if you want me to last the night."

"I hadn't really thought of dinner, sorry, Sav."

"It's all good, Jodi. Why don't we try that new wine and tapas bar in the city? I can get a feed, and we can start the night with cocktails, before we head somewhere to dance."

"Sounds like a good plan to me. I'll call a cab. You don't mind if I crash here, do you?"

"Nah, that's fine," I say, as I'm zipping up my boots.

While we are waiting for the cab, we have a few more shots...this is going to be one messy amazeballs night.

Jodi and I got back to my place just as the sun was coming up. It's midafternoon when I wake up and I feel like death warmed up. My head is pounding, my legs ache from dancing for hours on end, and I feel like I could vomit for Australia and take home the gold. Jodi is one wild child; I have not had that much fun in a longtime.

After going to the bathroom, I head to the lounge room to check on Jodi, but she is nowhere to be found. I head to the kitchen for a much needed glass of water and a huge coffee. I have just turned on my coffee machine when I get a text.

Jodi – *Thanks for a great night, mole. I haven't danced like that in sooooo long. We have to do it again. See you at work tonight*

Me – *With how I feel right now not sure I will make it to work tonight. Definitely have to do it again*

Jodi – *Bitch, you better be there*

Me – *Yes, Mum. See you tonight*

After my coffee, water, and Advil, I head back to bed for more sleep; hopefully I'll feel human when I wake up. I set my alarm so I'm not late for work. I fall into a deep sleep where a certain baldheaded hottie makes an appearance.

I walk into work and the first person I see is Jodi. She looks fresh as a daisy, and I wonder how she does it. I still feel and look like shite. She looks up, and when she sees me, she starts laughing. I give her the finger as I head out back and sign in.

The night flies by as it is super busy, due to a big footy game in town tonight. I'm thankful it went fast. I knock off just after midnight, and as I'm leaving, I find myself sad that Mike didn't come in tonight.

13

MIKE

It's Saturday afternoon and I'm over at Kenzie and Jordan's for a new tasting session. Normally, I'm all over these sessions. but my heart just isn't in it today, plus I still get judgey eyes from a few of the Malt Me employees. Obviously some still hold me responsible for De-Niece, and I really can't blame them. I still blame me, too.

Don't get me wrong, I'm happy to spend time one-on-one with Kenz, Jordan, and the twins but not in a group like this, it's still too soon. Thankfully the baby monitor goes off.

"I swear, my girls have perfect timing, I'll be right back," Kenz says, as she puts her drink on the table. She stands up and kisses Jordan on the cheek before heading inside. Seeing them, for a fleeting moment, I wish I had something like them, but then I remember that chicks are nothing but trouble and the feeling passes.

"Let me help you, Kenz, besides I haven't had Mac and Cheese cuddles for days. I'm sure they are missing their Unky Mike." Yes, I would rather deal with a shitty baby nappy than have everyone judge me.

"Seriously, stop calling them Mac and Cheese."

"Nope, nah, uh, not gonna happen. My lil' angles will always be Mac and Cheese to me, and until they tell me otherwise, the nickname stays." Kenz glares at me. "What are you gonna do, woman?"

"I'll...I'll cut off your beer supply."

"You wound me, Kenz." I push past her. "Come on and let's go see my girls."

We are just inside the patio doors when I slap Kenz on the ass for fun, and she squeals. I hear Jordan yell, "Keep your hands off my wife!"

We are both laughing. "Nope, not a chance, asshat." I quickly slam the patio door before he can whip my ass.

"Lucky I like you, Mike."

"Pfft, you love me, Kenz."

"Nope, pretty sure I love Jordan."

"You keep telling yourself that, Kenz baby, you're still in denial." I turn and face her, seductively rubbing my hands over my chest, swinging my hips as I sing, "You love me, you wanna kiss me."

"Yes, Mike, that must be it," she sarcastically replies, as she side steps me and heads towards the twins' bedroom.

We quietly poke our heads in, just in case they went back to sleep, but when we open the door, both of them are lying in their cots, playing with their toes. My face immediately lights up when I see them, these two totally have me wrapped around their little fingers, and I don't care that it makes me a total pussy.

Smiling, I look towards Kenz as she picks up Rory, and I head over to Indi's cot. "Kenz, you and Jordan sure make cute kids."

"Yeah, we do, don't we?"

"Modest much?" I say, as I bend down and pick up Indi. "Hey, Indi girl." And I give her a gentle kiss on her head. She looks up at me and goos, as she pulls on my goatee. Again, I can't help but smile. I'm lost in the cuteness that is Indi and don't realise that Kenz has changed Rory.

"Earth to Uncle Mike, you going to change her or just stare?"

In a goo-goo baby voice, I say, "Unky Mike can do it, can't he, Indi?" She blows a raspberry at me. "I'll take that as a yes." Turning towards the change table, I gently lay Indi down, as I'm pulling down the nappy cover thingy, she does the biggest fart, "On second thought, I'll have Rory cuddles. I don't do shit."

"You're such a pansy, Mike." Kenz hands me Rory and she changes Indi. Once they are both changed, we head to the kitchen to get their bottles. I'm a little upset that I don't get to see Kenzie's cans but I'll get to feed Rory, so I still win. Kenz and I head to the family room and we each feed the girls.

These two sweethearts are the apples of my eye; I can't wait until I have kids of my own. I get upset at this thought because I will never get that chance. I'm never having a girlfriend again. Kenz must sense my despair as when I glance up, she's looking intently at me. I know that a Kenzie lecture is not far away. No sooner have I finished that thought she starts.

"How you doing, Mike? And before you say fine, I know that's complete and utter horse shite."

"I'm...I really don't know how I'm doing, Kenz."

She gets up and comes to sit next to me. After she settles Indi back into her feed, she looks at me. "Spill, Mike Mustange, what's going on in that bald head of yours?"

"I'm just coasting along, Kenz. Nothing excites me anymore, I'm not even excited to be here today." Her head snaps up at that, "See, I'm in a funk." Pausing, I let out a sigh, "At times I still feel guilty. I know that you don't think it's my fault but, Kenz, I was literally fucking the enemy. How much of a chump was I to not know who she really was?"

"Mike, I have said this to you a million times. None of us knew; we were all clueless."

"I guess I just question my judge of character now." Reaching over I squeeze her hand. "Kenz, I will never forgive myself for what happened with De-Niece, but I'm just glad that I got there in time. I no longer feel guilty for killing her." Pausing, "I...I feel guilty for letting you and Jordan down."

"Mike, you didn't let us down. As you said, if it wasn't for you, who knows what would have happened? Now look at me, Mike."

I raise my head and look at Kenz, she has her *don't fuck with me* look on her face. "Now, I don't want to you dwell on that. I'm fine, Mac and Cheese are fine, Jordan is fine, and those fuckers are rotting in hell."

"You called them Mac and Cheese and you swore."

"Focus, Mike. Everyone who matters is fine, well,

you're not fine, but I'll get you there. There is no point in dwelling on what we can't change. All we can do is focus on the future AND that future will include you finding a lovely lady that I will allow around my munchkins."

"I hope you're right, Kenz."

"Of course I'm right, Mike. I'm always right."

"You're ohh so modest, too."

"And that's why you love me." She shrugs. "Now, let's get outside and join in the beer tasting."

We both stand and I one arm hug Kenz. "Thanks, Kenz. I appreciate the pep talk."

"Anytime, Mike, anytime. Now, let's go get our beer on."

Shaking my head and laughing, I say as we head back outside to join everyone, "Shit, you've been hanging around Jor too much. You even talk like him now."

Jordan walks over to us and grabs Rory out of my arms. "Well, when you crash into your soul mate, literally, it's bound to happen." He places a kiss on Kenz's temple and she smiles lovingly up at him.

"Fuck, you two make me sick. If love means that I have to hand in my man card, I'll happily stay single."

The rest of the afternoon flies by, and I actually enjoy myself once I let go of the guilt. As usual, Jordan has created some smashing beers. I cannot wait to have a Sunday arvo sesh and enjoy them at Malt Me.

14

KELVIN

THERE IS NO WAY IN HELL I AM LETTING THAT little bitch get away with this. It's been six months since she took off, and I'm no closer to finding her. I need to call in reinforcements. When I get my hands on her, and what's rightfully mine, I will not be held accountable for what happens.

Picking up my phone, I search Google and get the number that I need. Grabbing a bourbon, I dial the number, and get a voicemail asking me to leave my details. I leave a message and pour myself another drink.

No sooner have I sat down and my phone rings. "Yeah?"

"Well, you're a rude fucker, aren't you? I'm looking for Kelvin Jones"

"Yep, that's me."

"I understand you need me to find someone?"

"Yeah, I'm looking for my niece."

"Why not go to the cops if she's family?"

"Because I don't want the little bitch to know or hear

that I'm looking for her, it has to be a surprise when I find her. Your ad says you are discreet."

"That's right, she won't even know I'm there."

"That's perfect then. You're hired."

"I never said I'd do it."

"What?"

"You seem like a pompous asshole. I'm not sure I want to work for someone like you. Besides, how do I know you can afford me?"

"Do you think I would call you if I couldn't afford it? I'm not stupid."

"You're lucky that I need the money so I'll take the job. My fee is five hundred per day, plus accommodation. Now, give me as much information as you can about your niece."

"Fuck, that's steep."

"It is what it is, now do you want me or not?"

"Fine, but I'm pretty sure you are ripping me off. The bitch's name is Savannah 'Sav' Blac. Family owns the Blac Family Jewelers chain. She recently sold a house in Wentworthville. That's all I know."

"Age and description would also help."

"She's twenty-something, fucked if I'd know. She has amazing blue eyes like my late sister, blonde hair, legs that go on forever."

"Enough, send me through a photo. As soon as I receive a four-day advance and her photo, I'll get started. I'll give you a daily update."

"You better find her, it's important."

"They all say it's important. I'll be in touch."

Hanging up, I sigh. *Fuck this is going to cost me a*

fortune, I think to myself as I scroll through my phone to send him a photo of Sav. After making the payment, I text him her photo and proof of sending the money.

Kelvin – *Proof of payment and photo*
James – *Thanks. I'll send an update when I have something*
Kelvin – *Don't waste my time, asshole*

Sitting down after pouring another drink, I sigh. *Why the fuck is this happening to me?* Can't believe this is what my life has become, things were much easier before.

Sipping my drink, I think how much better life will be when I get my hands on the jackpot. It should have been mine in the first place, but no, Miss I'm Daddy's Princess had to fuck it all up. Well, who's laughing now? Me, that's who, and when I finally get what's mine, there will be no stopping me.

15

MIKE

THERE'S A NEW BAR WENCH AT THE DUNGEON AND she is fucking stunning. I can't get her off my mind. Savannah Blac, what the fuck are you doing to me? She's my last thought at night when I go to sleep. She's the first thing I think about when I wake up. When I'm making coffee at work, she's on my mind. She has totally consumed my life, and apart from me asking for a beer or tequila shot or how's the weather, we haven't had a real conversation.

Her voodoo pussy has overtaken my mind and I'm fucked. I swore I would never go there again after the De-Niece debacle, but there is something about this girl. My force field is waning and I'm not sure how much longer I can deny myself. I need to get to know Savannah 'Sav' Blac and have her in my life.

I remember one Saturday afternoon when I walked in; I immediately spotted her behind the bar. She was squatting down, and when she stood up, I was lost in her sky blue eyes. When she turned around to get the tequila

I asked for, I nearly came in my pants; her ass was heaven. Her black work pants accentuated the curves, highlighting the prefect roundness. She must do a million squats a day to get that amazing curve. What I wouldn't give to squeeze her ass as she wraps herself around me and then sink my cock balls deep inside her. But I don't see that happening anytime soon. We outrageously flirted with each other, but she seemed hesitant to take it any further.

I need to stop thinking about the goddess named Savannah Blac!

———

I've agreed to meet Kenz at the Dungeon today for an afternoon sesh. Pretty sure she wants to meet up to give me another, "It's not your fault, pull your head out of your ass speech." Deep down I know it's not my fault, but I still feel like a piece of shit for not knowing that my girl-friend was a psycho, ho bag, bitch face, working with the douche canoe fuckface.

As I'm getting ready to meet Kenz, I ask myself the million dollar question: *How did I not know that I was fucking a fruitcake?* It's beyond me how I didn't know, and eight months later, I still feel like a fucking chump. Some how, Kenz and Jordan don't blame me but I don't care what they say. I'm partly to blame.

Looking up at my reflection in the mirror, I have an 'ahh ha' moment. It's time to get on with my life; I can't let the past, or that bitch, hinder my future. After all, I'm Mike Fucking Mustange and I'm fucking awesome.

Bending down, I put my boots on and think that maybe Sav is the girl for me. We get along well, we both like tequila, I'm hot, she's smokin' hot. She makes me smile and laugh, her ass is amazing, and she is the sexiest woman I've ever met. Nodding to myself, I decide that I really want to get to know this girl better, but first, I need to get Kenz off my back.

While I'm waiting for the cab, I decide that I will keep my Sav feelings a secret from Kenz. I'm still not one-hundred-percent sure that I want to go there yet, and if she finds out, she'll meddle like she always does. I can see it now, 'Operation Get Sav and Mike Together' will be put in motion, and I'm not quite ready to make that leap yet...or at all. Jeannie will be happy that I'm at least open to the subject now, that's a step forward in the right direction.

I'm running late, as usual, and I know she's going to be pissed. I won't have Jordan to defend me, as he is on daddy duty. It will just be Kenz and me, and to tell you the truth, I'm really looking forward to some one-on-one Kenz time. She and I haven't been out for drinks together in a long time, too long, in fact. I'm really looking forward to a messy tequila filled afternoon/night.

Finally, the cab turns up, and as I get in; I decide that tonight is the night, no more Mike woe-is-me Mustange. It's time for the return of Mike I'm-fucking-awesome Mustange.

16

KENZIE

THIS HAS GONE ON LONG ENOUGH; MIKE NEEDS TO
stop blaming himself. I thought after our chat at the tasting, he was on the mend, but he's still blaming himself.
Today is the day that it stops. *I'm on a mission.* Jordan is
going to watch the girls and I'm meeting Mike at The
Black Dungeon. We will eat wings, drink beer, sink
tequila shots, and I will finally get him to lose the guilt
over what happened. *'Mission Save Mike' is a go.* Jordan
agrees with me, so it was pretty easy to convince him. He
wants to see Mike happy and himself again, just as much
as I do.

As usual, Mike is late, but I strike up a conversation
with this awesome bartender. Her name is Sav; she's
newish to town. We hit it off immediately, and I think
that now that Sarah is preoccupied, she could be my new
partner in crime. Thinking of Sarah I start to feel sad,
something is up with her, and once I have Mike back on
track, she will be next on my fix list.

I've just ordered another beer, thinking about what's

going on with Sarah, when Mike finally walks in. I must say, he is looking mighty fine this afternoon, actually he generally does. Today he is wearing his Wrangler jeans and black button-down shirt; and just for me, he's wearing his black Johnny Reb ankle boots. If I weren't happily married to Jordan, I'd totally do him.

"Looking good, Mr. Mustange," I say, jumping up to give him a hug and kiss on the cheek. As I'm releasing Mike, I notice that the bar chick is seething at our hug, and I notice Mike checking her out too. This totally changes the path of 'Mission Save Mike.' I cannot wait to put it into action.

"Mrs. McRoberts, as usual, you look stunning. Why could it not have been me you smashed into, all those years ago?" He slaps me on the ass, before taking a seat next to me at the bar; we both start laughing. He nod's towards Sav to bring him a beer and I notice that she seems pissed...towards me all of a sudden. She and I were getting along so well when I first got here. *Interesting*, I think to myself when I notice that she's flirting with Mike, and he's flirting back.

"You couldn't handle me, dude." Taking a swig of my beer before adding, "Besides, I prefer dudes with hair on their head, and not their chin." Reaching over, I tug on his goatee as I say this.

We are both laughing as Sav places a beer in front of Mike, and I say, "Sav, can you please bring me another beer and four shots of Jose, please? My buddy, Mike, here, needs a swift mummy talk and Jose is needed for this conversation." Raising my eyebrows, I wink at Mike.

Sav turns to get our drinks and I yell, "Can you also add a portion of hot wings and sliders, please?"

Noticing her demeanor change when I mention that Mike is a friend, *I'm so onto something*, I think to myself. Mike and I start talking about Jordan and the girls. When she comes back, she happily hands me my beer, and effortlessly pours six shots and replies, "Can do, Kenz, and since you're stuck with this guy." She points and wiggles, her finger at Mike. "Here's an additional two...on me."

Smiling, I swiftly reply, "Fuck, I love you. We so need to hang out, remind me to give you my details before I leave tonight." Sav nods, before turning and serving the others at the bar.

From the corner of my eye, I notice Mike inwardly groan and cringe at my encounter with Sav, and I totally know that I'm onto something here. There's definite chemistry between them, AND they have both been, not so discreetly, checking each other out.

'Mission Save Mike' just keeps getting better and better.

17

MIKE

Walking in, I immediately see Sav is working. My heart rate increases, I feel happy, and my cock starts to twitch at her beauty. I see her hand Kenz a beer, *that's my girl*, I think to myself as I walk up to her. "Mrs. McRoberts, as usual you look stunning. Why could it not have been me you smashed into, all those years ago?" Winking at her, I slap her ass as I sit down at the bar next to her. Waving my arm, I grab Sav's attention and order a beer, and another for Kenz; she's a guzzler.

Kenz snort-laughs when I smack her ass and I can't help but smile a real smile, I haven't had a real smile on my face in a long time. Kenz really brings out the best in me, and after all these years, her snort-laugh still sets me off. Taking a sip of my beer, I look over to Kenz, who is also smiling. She winks at me, and I know that we are going to have a great, but messy, evening together. *Bring it on!*

It's almost closing time and Kenz and I are plastered, like shitfaced, can hardly stand plastered. Together we have had up-deen-dozen shots, a gazillion beers, four million wings and a fantabolous time.

I've noticed Sav giving me weird looks tonight. I don't know what's up, and every time I go to ask Sav, Kenz grabs my attention and I get sidetracked. *I hope I haven't pissed her off and ruined my chance before I've even got it.*

Sav calls last drinks, and Kenz and I grab another round of shots and one final beer chaser. She's going to be feeling this tomorrow, but it was so much fun, we need to do this again. We've just finished our drinks and stand up to leave. Kenz wobbles around the bar and whispers something to Sav. Walking back to me, she links our arms and as we are leaving, turns to Sav and says, "See you next Wednesday."

After standing around outside, for what feels like forever, a cab finally pulls up. Jumping in with Kenz, I get the cabbie to drop Kenz off first and then me; I'm not waiting another billion minutes. We get to Kenz and Jordan's place, and I see her to the door. Jordan meets us and just shakes his head at me and smart-assly says, "Thanks for looking after my wife, I told you, no shots."

Bursting out laughing, I reply, "You've met your wife, try telling her no, or 'you've had enough'. Besides, she was a few beers in by time I arrived. But seriously, dude, thanks for letting me have her tonight. It was just what I needed." I see Jordan smile in appreciation, just as Kenz vomits on the front verandah. "And, on that note, I'm out of here. See you Wednesday for Origin."

Jordan shouts, "Thanks, asshole, see you Wednesday!"

Waving, I turn and race back to the cab. Before I

know it, we are pulling into my driveway. I pay the cabbie and I head inside, stripping off before collapsing onto my bed and falling into a deep and drunken slumber.

For the first time in months, I easily fall to sleep and don't dream. My chat with Kenz this evening was just what I needed and only cemented my new outlook on what happened and life in general. Finally, I agree that I'm not to blame, but I still feel like a chump. I'm just as much of a victim as she and Jordan. When I wake the next morning, I decide that I'm taking my life back; Mike Mustange is back, people.

18

SAV

WHO THE FUCK IS THIS CHICK ALL OVER MIKE? BUT more so, why the fuck do I care? He's just a baldheaded, uber hottie who comes in here, he has a heart of gold, and he's fun to be around. From the bits he has said, I can tell he's going through something rough, and that's enough for me to keep my distance. I don't need more drama, I left to get away from it and I don't need that here...but I can't get Mike Mustange off my mind.

Looking up, I see him smiling and that, in turn, makes me smile; he has this voodoo effect on my pussy. Hence why, at the moment, he is the main attraction of my nighttime fantasies; poor Buzz. *Buzz is going to die at the rate I'm using him at the moment.*

I know I'm meant to be lying low until I'm sure Uncle Kelvin given up his quest to get what is supposedly his, but there is something about this guy that has me hooked. The nights he doesn't come in, I find myself sad, but as soon as I see him walk in, my face lights up and my body reacts to the sight of him in a way that I have never felt before. I imagine what it would be like to be under him as he pounds into me, my legs wrapped tightly around him, holding him closer, so he can get in deeper.

My night gets better when I realise that his friend, is actually is just, his friend. Kenz and I chat throughout the night and I really like her. We hit it off immediately and swap numbers to catch up again.

When Mike ducked to the loo, she asked me to their annual Origin party next week. Immediately, I said that I'd love to go but I'm not sure I should, since I'm a New South Wales supporter and we are in Queensland. But Kenz seems awesome and I'm lonely. I'd love to make another friend, and as an added bonus, I get to see Mike outside of work. Is it bad that I'm more excited about that than I am about gaining a friend?

———

It's finally starting to feel like home here. Don't get me wrong, I miss my friends from Wentworthville, and I feel bad that I haven't kept in touch, but I had to get away from Uncle Kelvin. Even all these months later, I'm not sure I'm strong enough face him again.

Most of all, it's nice to just blend in and not have anyone know my history. I couldn't stand the sad pitying looks anymore, but here I have a clean slate and no one knows about my tragically sad past. Here I'm Sav Blac, new girl in town. Where as back home, I was Sav Blac, poor orphan girl.

Another person to make me happy is Mike Mustange. Fuck, he's hot, like panty-melting hot, but he looks sad and lost; kind of like me. There is something about him that I'm drawn to; he's an enigma that I want to crack open. Even though I don't really know him, he makes me smile; he makes me happy and not sad. This happiness only occurs when he is around but his sadness scares me.

I'm finally in a good place and I don't want him to ruin this. I don't want anything to ruin my happiness. But there is something about him that I'm drawn to. I'm like a moth to a flame when it comes to Mike Mustange. I want to throw caution to the wind and just go for it, but I'm a total chicken and can't.

I'll just keep admiring his ohh-so-fucking-fine form from a distance—sigh. What I wouldn't give to have those muscular tattooed arms wrapped around me as I hold him close to my body. My breasts pushed up against his chest as I stare into his sky blue eyes...ohh well, looks like I'll just be imagining it's him when I give B.O.B. a work out...again.

After such a long shite period, things are finally looking up for me.

19

KELVIN

I'T'S BEEN ALMOST TWO WEEKS AND JAMES IS NO closer to finding Sav. It's really pissing me off. I'm already down five G's and there is no end in sight. This asshole better come up with something other than, "I'm working on a lead," or "I'm close." Maybe I need to pull him and get someone else to do it.

Walking into The Grand Hotel for a pub feed and beer, I take a seat at the bar and start to calm down. The ice-cold beer is just what I need, I can feel the yeasty goodness starting to relax me. Smiling, I order another beer when my phone rings. I don't feel like talking but when I see it's James, I answer.

"Hello, James."

"Kelvin, I have good news."

"I'll be the judge of that."

"You're such an asshole" Pausing for effect, he continues, "Maybe I'll just keep my find to myself then."

Standing up, I head outside, as I don't want anyone hearing this conversation. "Like fuck you will, I'm paying you here, asshole, now stop fucking around and tell me."

"I found her."

Silence, I'm stunned that he actually came through for me. "Come again?"

"I found your niece, Sav Blac is working bar in Brisbane, Queensland."

"Well fuck a duck, you actually found the little bitch. I started to think you were leading me up the garden path."

"Listen here, you little weasel. I always come through, you go bad-mouthing me, and we will see who's the whiney little bitch. Now, I expect the balance to be in my account within the next twenty minutes. As soon as I have confirmation of the deposit, I will call you back with her address and place of employment, AND then I want you to lose this number. I never want to hear form you again."

"Fine by me."

Hanging up, I log into my banking and send the asshole his final payment, screen shot it, and text him. A few seconds later, my phone rings and he gives me the details on Sav. I pocket my phone, and smiling, I walk back inside, order another beer, and a Parma. This night cannot get any better.

While I'm waiting for my meal, I whip out my iPad and Google her location. After I have what I need, I look up where she works. "What a fucking dump," I mumble, "No surprises she'd work in a shithole." Now that I know where she is, I need to come up with a plan. It would be too easy to just contact her; I'm going to have some fun.

By the end of the night, I have it all worked out. Looks like I'm heading to Brisvegas...time for the fun to begin.

20

MIKE

THIS IS THE WEEK FROM HELL AND IT'S DRAGGING ever so slowly. All I can think about is Origin on Wednesday night and hanging with the gang. It feels like forever since we've all hung out together, and for once, I'm not feeling guilty. An added bonus is that I will get baby cuddles. Who knew I, Mike Mustange, would fawn over two teeny tiny adorable little munchkins, but when they are as cute as Mac and Cheese, it's not hard to.

Finally, it's Wednesday and I'm super excited for Origin tonight. The boss must have gotten laid last night, as he is in a really great mood and he let's us all leave early. Not giving him a chance to change his mind, I pack up and get out of there.

After leaving the office, I head to the gym for a workout before heading home to get organised for tonight. My workout lasted longer than I expected, so when I get home, I quickly grab a shower and get changed into my Queensland jersey, *Go Queensland,* I think as I pull it over my head, my well-worn R.M

Williams jeans, and broken in black chucks. Once I'm dressed, I call a cab and head outside to wait for it.

Ten minutes later, it arrives and I give him Kenzie and Jordan's address; I also get him to stop in at the bottle-o since I didn't have time. Racing inside, I grab a carton of beer and a bottle on Pinot for Kenz. As usual, I'm running late and it's just after 7:00 p.m. before I arrive.

Opening the front door, while balancing the carton and wine, the first person I see when I look up is Sav. *What the fuck is she doing here?* Before my brain clicks in, I blurt out, "What the fuck are you doing here?" I immediately think, *Dickhead Mike,* so I quickly add, "And in a Blues shirt." *Nice save,* I think to myself.

Kenz walks over, punches me in the arm and says, "Don't be rude, Mike. I invited her so be nice. Besides, it's not her fault she goes for the wrong team." She winks at Sav before grabbing the wine and heading into the kitchen.

Walking inside, I place the carton on the island bench and walk over to Sav, who by this point is looking really uncomfortable, and I feel like an ass for making her feel like that. "Hey, Sav. Sorry about that, I just wasn't expecting you to be here."

She hesitantly looks at me and replies, "I can go, if you'd prefer?"

"No, please stay." I panic at the thought of her leaving and I really want her to stay. Leaning over I whisper, "Besides if you leave, Kenz will ride my ass, and she's dangerous when she's pissed off."

WHACK

Rubbing my arm; I turn around to see Kenz there, holding a beer for me and glass of wine for Sav.

"I heard that, asshole, no brownies for you later." She hands us our drinks, and adds, "Sav, please ignore this asshat. He doesn't know when, or how, to behave."

Jordan comes over and hands Kenz her wine/ "Hey, Mike, I see you are in fine form this evening."

"What is it, pick on Mike night?"

In unison, Kenz and Jordan reply, "Yep!"

Sav laughs, and says, "I'd love to stay." Pausing she looks intently at me and adds, "Plus I can't wait to see New South Wales kick your ass."

Kenz, Jordan, and I all burst out laughing. I look over at Sav and in between laughs I declare. "Keep dreamin', babe, keep dreamin'."

Sav smirks, takes a sip of wine, points at me. "Okay, Mr. Queensland, let's make a bet. If New South Wales wins, you have to do anything that I suggest."

"...And when Queensland wins? What do I get?"

"Whatever you decide, but we need to decide here and now, so it's all on the table."

"Okay, when Queensland wins, you have to go on a date with me." *Where the fuck did that suggestion come from?* I look over and notice Sav's cheeks have flushed, and she looks towards the floor with a smile on her face.

Looking back up at me shyly, she asks, "You want a date with me? Really?"

"Yeah, why not?"

Sav pushes her hand out. "Deal."

I spit in my hand and shake her outstretched one. Her skin is silky smooth, and I immediately picture her hand wrapped around my cock, squeezing tight as she strokes up and down. Shaking my head, and discreetly adjusting my cock, I say, "Deal."

"Eeww, did you seriously just spit and shake my hand?"

"Ah, yeah, sorry about that. I'm used to doing deals with Jordan, and we've been spitting on it since we were ten years old." I walk over to the TV cabinet and grab a tissue, turning around; I grab her hand and gently wipe off my spit. Her hand feels so good in mine and my touch lingers longer than it should.

Looking up, I see Sav smiling and it makes me smile. She pulls her hand back and I long to have her hand in mine once again. "Thanks, Mike, I've got it."

"No worries, Sav. Again, sorry bout that. Promise on our next bet that I won't spit." She smiles at me again and a rush of happiness courses through me, smiling back I ask, "So, what do I have to do for you when you don't win?"

"Well, when I win, you have to help me paint my duplex."

"Okay, I can handle that, but it's not gonna happen, so don't get too excited. Queensland has it in the bag."

"We'll see," she cheekily replies, before taking a sip of her wine. "This wine is divine, what is it?"

"Huh, that rhymes. Umm, it's a New Zealand one that I can't pronounce from the Marlborough region." Again, I find myself smiling, looking over I notice a sad looking Kenz walking back down the hallway. Walking over to her, I pull her in tight for a sideways hug. "What's up, baby girl?"

"That was Sarah, she's stuck at work and can't make it, but I know it's a lie. She's holding back on me."

"What makes you say that?"

"Her voice gets high-pitched when she lies and her pitch was opera worthy just then. She also quickly hung up on me. When have you ever known her to not want to talk? Even if she was at work."

"Maybe she's having an off night, is Josh not coming too then?"

"We never mentioned Josh, but I think they are having trouble. I haven't seen him in forever."

"Ohh well, more wings for me then. The four of us can still have a footytabolous evening, though." Everyone laughs and we settle in the media room just as the game begins.

———

The four of us have a great night and for the first time in forever, New South Wales fucking wins, and I'm now going to be at Sav's mercy. She has an evil glint in her eye; I'm scared.

Getting up to get another round of drinks, I hesitantly ask, "So, Sav, when does my punishment happen?"

"Wouldn't you like to know?"

"Seriously, when do you want me?"

"I don't want you, I just want your body." I'm left standing there open-mouthed at what she said. She quickly adds, "I want your body for painting. Ummm, be at my place at 10:00 a.m. Saturday, does that work for you?"

"Sounds good to me, Sav. Do you need me to bring anything?"

"Nah, just yourself. Actually you better bring a change of clothes, too." She heads over to Kenz and they open another bottle of wine. I'm left standing there, kind of stunned...and totally horny. Why do I need a change of clothes? Hmm, this could be interesting.

I'M SUCH AN EVIL COW, USING MIKE LIKE THIS, BUT the way he reacted when he arrived really pissed me off. If I'm being totally honest, it cut me deep, real deep, and that surprised me.

Mike and I agreed to meet at 10:00 a.m. to get the duplex painted, I failed to mention that it is only the lounge room that we are painting, so he should be happy. I'm really happy that my landlord said it was okay to repaint, this place will finally feel like home after I do that.

She totally blew me away when she offered to pay for it; her only stipulation was no shitty colours. To appease her, I agreed to meet at the paint shop so she could help choose. Earlier in the week, we met up at the paint place and agreed on a colour. She paid for everything and I left with all that I needed to get the job done.

It's just before 10:00 a.m. when Mike arrives, and I can't help but smile. He has a tray of coffees and a huge box with him. I take the coffees from him and he follows me into the kitchen. He places the box on the kitchen bench and I take a peek inside, there is every kind of cake in there. My mouth immediately waters. Looking up, I see Mike staring at me, and my cheeks heat when he grins at me. As usual when I'm around him, I find myself smiling. I've noticed that I always am when Mike is around.

"What's all this?"

"Food," he smartly replies.

"No shit, Sherlock, are we expecting the Queensland team to come and help? There's enough food here for the entire squad."

"Ha, no just us. Painting works up an appetite so I thought I'd come prepared, plus I wasn't sure what your cake of choice was."

He passes me a coffee, our fingers grazing as he hands it to me. The world around us ceases to exist; it's just Mike and me. The spark from our fingers touching, jolts right through me, the electric zap that occurs would be enough to light a small country town for weeks. My insides clench and my cheeks turn pink as my mind runs wild with dirty thoughts. I'm brought back to reality when I Mike says, "Your skinny salted caramel latte, with two sugars."

My smile widens, when I realise that he brought me my coffee, exactly how I like it. "Why thank you, but don't think you will be getting out of painting just because you bought coffee and a sugar coma with you."

"A guy's gotta try." He winks before adding, "At least we're only painting the lounge room, I was dreading doing the whole place and with that huge front window, it's just three walls. It will be easy as. We should have the under coast and first coat done today and be finished tomorrow."

"How did you know it was just the lounge room?"

"Kenz let it slip."

"Well, no more free tequila for her when she comes into work."

"What about free tequila for me?"

"Depends on how good of a painter you are," I cheekily reply.

"For free tequila, I'll smash this painting out and you'll be amazed. Just you wait and see."

"Mmhmm, we'll see." I bring my cup up to my lips and I take a sip of my coffee; I close my eyes and enjoy this liquid gold as it hits my taste buds. "Man, Mike, this coffee is to die for. I need to know where you got it from."

"A coffee shop." Winking at me, as he also takes a sip.

"No shit, Sherlock, which coffee shop?"

"Java Lava."

"Is that the one next to Stratton College?"

"Yeah, that's the one, it's totally out of the way from anywhere, but ever since college, I always get my coffee from there."

"Looks like I have a new coffee shop. What are their brownies like?"

"They are pretty good, not as good as Kenzie's though. She makes a killer brownie."

"I know, those ones on Wednesday were to die for."

We take our coffees to the front verandah and chat. It's so comfortable and feels like we have known each other for years. There are no awkward silences and we have even finished each other's sentences on a few occasions. I don't know if it's wishful thinking, but I think Mike is flirting with me, and I really like it when he does.

Just as we are finishing our coffees, I get the feeling someone is watching me. I discretely look around but don't see anything out of the ordinary. Once inside, I place the coffee cups into the bin and we get into the painting.

Mike was right, we get the under coat and first coat done by midafternoon, and we decide to call it a day. He agrees to meet back here at the same time tomorrow.

Walking Mike to the door, we say goodbye, and I give him a kiss on the cheek. Pulling back, I look up at Mike and see lust in his eyes. Before it goes any further, I take a step back. "Thanks for your help today, Mike, I don't think I would have got this done by myself."

"Happy to help, Sav. Besides, a bet's a bet." He turns, opens the front door, and looks over his should as he walks out saying, "Night, lovely lady, see you tomorrow morning."

"Bye, Mike." I close and lock the screen. I feel sad and lonely now that he's gone. As I walk to the bathroom, I realise that once again after being around Mike, I'm smiling and happy.

Deciding to have a bath and chillax, I grab a bottle of wine and begin filling the bathtub when I get a text. It's from an unknown number.

Unknown – *I'll see you soon*

Without thinking, I delete it; it must be a wrong

number. Just as I put the phone down another text comes through.

Mike – *I had fun today*

My heart flutters as I read his text, and a wave of euphoric happiness washes over my body. *I had fun today, too*, I think to myself; actually it's the most fun I've had in a longtime.

Sav – *I had fun too. Thanks for all your help. See you tomorrow*

Placing my phone back on the counter, I grab a wine glass and head into the bathroom. Lighting a few candles, I climb into the tub, immerse myself in the jasmine-scented bubbles, and relax.

Once the water turns cold, I climb out, put on my navy satin, knee-length nightie, turn on *Netflix,* and get absorbed watching the Winchester boys fight demons on *Supernatural.* It's just before midnight when I climb into bed; my last thoughts before I fall into slumber are of Mike.

The next morning, just after 10:00 a.m., Mike arrives and before we get stuck into the painting, we again have coffee on the verandah. Just like yesterday, he stopped at Java Lava on his way over, and this time he got a brownie for me and banana bread for him. The conversation flows, it is comfortable and nice and I find myself smiling and deliriously happy.

Looking up, I see Mike staring at me. "What?"

Wiping my mouth before I add, "Do I have something on my face?"

Mike laughs at me, "Nope, nothing on your face. It's just nice to see your real smile and not the fake one."

"I do not have a fake smile."

He scrunches up the paper bag his banana bread came in and throws it at me. "Yeah, you do." My reflexes aren't the best and it collects the side of my head. I sit there, shake my head in shock. I look over at Mike and we both burst out laughing.

"Wow, you were right when you said you were unco."

"I'm not unco, I'm just not all that coordinated."

"Yes, the definition of unco."

He takes a sip of his coffee and I watch him swallow, his Adam's apple moving ever so seductively as the coffee makes its way down. All of a sudden there's a pulsating sensation between my legs, and I'm pretty sure my cheeks heat as well.

Quickly I stand up and head inside, I'd hate for Mike to know what I'm thinking. "I'm heading inside to get started, you finish your coffee and come in when you're done."

As I'm squeezing past, Mike suddenly stands up, we bump each other and he reaches his hand out to steady me. We stand there staring into each other's eyes; the heat radiating from his touch is scorching. Time stands still as the rest of the world fades away. Taking a deep breath, my tongue darts out and I lick my lip before biting on it. I realise that Mike is still holding my arm and we continue to stare intently at each other. There's an electric current fusing us together, neither of us wanting to break the connection.

Reaching up, he pushes a lock of hair behind my ear; the movement causes me to come to my senses. Pulling away, I quietly say, "Sorry, I guess I am unco."

Turning, I quickly race inside with my heart beating faster than I have ever felt it before. As I open the door, I think to myself, *What the fuck was that?*

22

MIKE

I'm standing on Sav's front patio and I'm staring at her as she races inside. *What the hell just happened?* One minute we are chatting, the next was like a scene from a movie.

Time stood still.

The only noise was the erratic beating of our hearts.

And in the blink of an eye, she's running off.

I'm at a loss as to what I should do. Do I go inside and demand we talk about it? Or do I just play dumb and leave it be? *God, where's Kenz when I need advice?*

As I walk inside, I'm thinking about the moment we just had. I know she felt what I felt and I guess that's why she ran off quickly. Looking at her, I decide that I don't want to spook her, so I play it safe and go with her; it never happened. *I must have imagined it.*

This is tough, I've sworn black and blue I will never have another girlfriend, but right at this moment, I want something with Sav. I want everything with Sav. If she pushes me away, or doesn't want this, I'll be devastated.

Pulling up my big boy pants, I take a deep breath and continue inside.

When I get inside, Sav is nowhere to be seen. My heart sinks, until I see her walk down the hallway. She pauses midstep when she sees me, but her eyes also light up at the same time. It gives me hope until her sweet angelic voice says, "Let's get this finished."

My heart sinks; I guess she isn't feeling what I'm feeling, after all. With a fake smile I mumble, "Yep, ah, sure, no worries."

We get straight into painting. Sav turns up the music, and I get the hint that this conversation is over...before it even began.

In no time at all, we have finished painting and the place looks amazing, Sav and I make a great team. Thankfully, our little encounter from this morning hasn't had an impact on our relationship...or whatever this is.

We have just cleaned up the last of the paint supplies, and I start moving Sav's furniture back into place. I've just positioned the couch, when Sav walks in and I pause, she looks stunning the in afternoon light. The rays of sunshine on her golden locks create a halo effect, turning her into an angel: *my angel*, I think to myself.

My cock hardens at her beauty and before I can say anything, she turns and heads into the kitchen. To hide my growing cock, I take a seat on her couch and adjust myself. Sighing as I sink into the lounge, it feels good to finally sit down. Closing my eyes, I lean back and relax, I also think of Grandma naked, to get my cock to go down.

Sav is taking a while, and I start to think that maybe

she wants me to leave when I hear her clear her throat. Opening my eyes, I see her standing next to the coffee table with a jug of beer and two ice-cold beer mugs.

Smiling, I curiously ask. "What's all this?"

She takes a seat next to me and I grab the jug, pouring us each a glass of beer. Handing her a beer, she says, "Well, I wanted to say thanks for helping with the painting, so I asked Jordan for a mini keg of your fav Malt Me beer. I've also ordered Chinese from Kung Fu Palace and there's salted caramel Tim Tams in the fridge for dessert."

"You seriously did all of this..." pausing, I can't believe she has done all of this, "...for me?"

"Yep. I really appreciate your help, Mike. If you hadn't help me, I would still be painting." Taking a sip of beer, she adds, "I really appreciate it."

She places her beer back on the coffee table and a lone tear cascades down her cheek, lowering her head she looks towards her lap.

Without thinking I reach over, lift her chin up, and I wipe away the tear with the pad of my thumb. Cupping her face with my palm, I run my thumb gently along her jaw line; she leans into my open palm and exhales. "Why are you crying, Sav?"

"I'm just...I'm just really thankful for your help. Not since...never mind, let's have a beer to celebrate my newly decorated lounge room."

"I'm down with having a beer, on the proviso that you tell me why you were crying and are now clearly upset."

Sav leans forward, grabs her beer, and chugs it back in one mouthful. She pours herself another and looks towards me. She smiles sadly and takes a deep breath. "My parents and brother were killed in a car accident earlier this year."

"Holy fucking shit, I'm so sorry, Sav."

"Don't be. I hate the pity I get from people when they find out, which is why I haven't told anyone here. I got overwhelmed just now, because if Jace were still alive, he and I would have done this together." She wipes away a stray tear and smiles. "Actually, he probably, no definitely, would have been my roommate. Mike, he wasn't just my brother, he was my best friend." She takes a breath; the tears are now steadily flowing down her cheeks. "I miss them so much, Mike. Some days, I wish I was with them, too. It hurts so fucking much."

Reaching over, I wrap my arms around her and console her. She snuggles into me as the sobs overtake her. I tighten my arms around her and rub her back in circles, like I've seen Jordan do with Kenzie when she's really upset.

We stay sitting like this for a while, her sobs have subsided but she's still emotional. I realise that I like this, having Sav in my arms. It feels right, not awkward, like she was made for me. We fit together perfectly, like two pieces of an intricate puzzle.

She pulls away from me and immediately I'm sad at the loss of her in my arms, but she smiles and it takes my breath away. No longer is it a sad smile, but it's a genuine Sav smile, and as usual when I'm around her, I find myself genuinely smiling too.

"Thanks, Mike."

"No need to thank me, Sav. I'm here anytime, day or night."

"You are too good to be true. Good-looking, nice, funny, and you love tequila. I'm glad to have met you, Mike Mustange."

"You think I'm good-looking?" I tease.

Her cheeks turn a pretty shade of pink; she's flustered as she replies, "I...I never said you were good-looking."

"Yeah, you did. And I quote 'Good-looking, nice, funny' and then something about tequila but I was hooked on the good-looking part. Care to elaborate further?"

"You, sir, are delusional. I said you were a good guy an..." Before she can finish there is a knock at the door. "That will be dinner." She eagerly says as she jumps up.

I mumble to myself, *"Fucking delivery guy."*

"Just 'cause dinner is here, doesn't mean this conversation is over."

"Whatevs. And yes, this conversation is over: done, dusted, kaput, the end, credits rolling. Moving on."

Sav answers the door and the heavenly scent of Kung Fu Palace permeates the air, I smile and groan. She pays the delivery guy and brings the food over. While she unpacks it, I head to the kitchen to get sporks and top up our jug.

As I'm refilling the jug, I smile. I'm blown away that she did all this...no one has ever done anything like this for me before. It makes me happy knowing she went out of her way arranging this. I know I'm going to sound like a girl, or Jordan, but I feel giddy and my heart is racing. Maybe, just maybe, I can explore what happened this morning further, but I'm not going to push her.

She was pretty upset when she was telling me about her family; I can't imagine what she's gone through. I'm not that close to Mum and Dad, but I still think it would suck. I guess I do know what she's going through, in a way. With all the shit that happened with Kenz and Jordan, I'd be lost without them.

"Dude, you better not be eating the Tim Tams, or worse, drinking all the beer."

Laughing, I close the fridge and head back into the lounge room. "Holy shit, are you feeding an army? You do realise there are only two of us, right?"

"Yeah, I did kinda go overboard but Fung Fu Palace is the bomb, and there's always leftovers."

"Pfft, leftovers. Woman, watch a learn."

We settle in, stuff our faces with food, and have a great night together. Sav shares a little more about her family but I get the feeling she's still holding back. I guess I don't blame her; it's hard opening up, and to a relative stranger, it would be even harder.

We have just cleaned up our mammoth meal, and I proved to Sav that Kung Fu Palace is no challenge for me. I'm actually impressed with all that I've eaten. I won't tell her that I kind of feel sick but that's my secret to keep.

She has poured us another beer and we are chatting about anything and everything. I've really gotten to know Sav tonight, and the more I know, the more I really like her. I'm tempted to break my no girlfriend rule when she stands up suddenly. I think that she is going to ask me to leave, as it's getting late. Instead she skips to the kitchen, returning with a bottle of tequila, two shot glasses, and my promised Tim Tams.

"Oh My God! Sav, you are the best. Marry me now."

My comment causes her to trip, the tequila slides across the chaise of the couch, and she falls onto my lap. Giggling, she looks up into my eyes, and before I have a chance to see if she's okay, her mouth is plastered to mine. Her tongue pushing for access and I hear her quietly moan.

Willingly, I open my mouth and our tongues wrestle. I pull her so she is straddling my hips, my hands grabbing her perfect ass, pulling her closer to me. She grinds herself on my cock and it immediately hardens. She's rocking back and forth as my hands work their way up her back.

Gently caressing her neck and shoulders, I pull her tighter to me and deepen the kiss. We both moan at the same time, Sav pulls back and rests her forehead against mine. I see indecision in her eyes, but before I can say anything, she pulls her singlet over her head. She's not wearing a bra, and at eye level are her perfectly pert, pink hard nipples, the sight before me is heavenly.

Leaning forward, I take her pink nub into my mouth and suck; she throws her head back in ecstasy as I suckle harder. With one hand, I massage her other breast. It fits perfectly in the palm of my hand. I squeeze her nipple before I suck on it, and I start to massage that one I had previously been sucking.

Sav continues to grind herself on my cock, and if she doesn't stop, I'm going to come in my pants. I wrap my arms around her and stand up, I place her onto the chaise and I squat between her open legs. Ever so slowly, I run my hands up her calf and thigh, before skimming my palm over her mound. I grip the top of her shorts and undies before stripping her naked.

I groan when I see her bare pussy glistening with her arousal. I lazily run my finger around her navel before sliding it down to her clit. I give it a flick before running my finger up and down, spreading her wetness. Slipping my finger inside, she exhales the breath she had been holding; her pussy is warm and inviting.

Watching Sav writhe in pleasure as she rides my hand is so hot. I insert another finger, plunging them in and out of her tight pussy; her moans getting louder and louder, her thrusts faster and faster. Leaning forward, I nibble on her bottom lip before sliding my tongue into her mouth. Her pussy walls tighten around my fingers, and I know she's going to come soon. I continue to kiss her as I insert a third finger. I feel her body shudder around my fingers, as she sucks the life out of my tongue. Never have I been so turned on watching another person come.

Removing my fingers, I sit up and I lick them clean. "Fuck, Sav, you taste amazing." Sav is still laying there, her breaths still labored and she looks stunning. Her pussy begging for more, I lower my head and suck her clit into my mouth before licking down her slit. "Oh my God! Your pussy is divine."

My tongue continues to dart in and out of her entrance, before I suck and nibble on her clit. She arches her back, and she starts to tweak her nipples, shoving my face further into her pussy. I suck on her swollen nub, before inserting a finger into her wet folds. Slipping my hand under her ass, I spread her juices over her tight hole, before I insert the tip of my pinkie into her ass.

Sav moans in pleasure as I push my finger further into her ass, when I insert my thumb into her pussy she screams, "Ohh, Mike!" as her second orgasm of the night rips through her body. Her body shudders as the pleasure courses from head to toe.

Gazing up, I see Sav looking down at me. Her cheeks flushed from two successive orgasms and the biggest smile I have ever seen on her face. Even though I haven't come yet, I have never felt such happiness before, and I smile back at her.

All of a sudden Sav tries to cover herself. I grab her hands, entwining our fingers, still sitting between her legs. "What do you think you're doing?"

"Well, umm, I'm naked. I kind of feel exposed."

"Well, I like you exposed." I wink before adding, "You are so fucking beautiful, Sav."

Sitting back on my heels, I pull her to the edge and kiss her. Our lips are gently caressing each other; I'm lost in the emotion of this kiss. When I pull back, I rest my forehead against hers and gaze at her and smile.

My lips are tingling, actually my whole body is prickling; I'm dizzy with lust. *I love kissing Savannah Blac*, I think to myself, before I lower my lips to her once again.

She deepens our kiss and wraps her legs around my waist, grinding herself on my growing erection. Wrapping my arms around Sav, I stand up and walk us down the hallway to her room.

Lowering her on the to bed, I stand up and quickly

remove my clothing. Settling myself between her legs before kissing her again. She drapes her arms over my shoulders, pulling me in closer; the feel of her tits pressed against me is amazing.

She pushes me away and I think that she doesn't want this anymore, but she reaches into the top draw of her side table and grabs a condom. I pull back, take it from her, and quickly sheath my cock before I line it up with her entrance. Ever so slowly, I inch my dick into her pussy. Both of us growling at the sensation, never has a pussy felt so good wrapped around my cock.

Our pace quickens, the thrusts becoming stronger and deeper, our kisses frenzied as we lose ourselves in each other. Before I know it, I feel Sav's walls tighten around my cock and it sets me off. We both detonate in unison, shouting each other's name as we ride out our orgasm together.

I ease out of Sav and lay next to her, we both roll onto our sides and gaze at each other, panting. No words are said but our eyes say it all, we are both falling for each other.

Sav and I fall asleep, wrapped in each other's arms. My last thought before I drift off is that this feeling is nice and I don't ever want it to end.

For the first time in a long time, I feel happy and content, nothing could ruin this feeling right now...or so I thought.

23

SAV

WHEN I WAKE THE NEXT MORNING, I ACHE FROM head to toe, and I have never felt more alive. I don't think I have ever had that many orgasms in one night, and we're not talking ish ones; these were mind-blowing, body-shuddering, out of this world orgasms. Rolling over, I see Mike, snoring softly and my heart flutters. My eyes roam over his muscular back, but then I start to panic. This wasn't meant to happen; I'm supposed to be lying low, not getting laid. I can't bring Mike, or anyone, into my life until I know that Uncle Kelvin is gone for good. It's too dangerous for Mike to be in my life right now. *Fuck, fuck, fuckity, fuck, what have I done?*

Mike must know I'm awake because he reaches over and begins to massage my breast. Closing my eyes, I let out a moan; his hands on my body feel amazing. Quickly, I push his hand away, jump out of bed, and head into my ensuite; slamming the door behind me. *No, No, No, I can't let this happen, even though I really, really want to,* I think to myself, as I lean on the vanity. Hanging my head towards the floor, I let the tears fall down my cheeks.

The feelings and emotions coursing through me at the moment are out of control. I love what Mike and I experienced last night, If I was in another situation, I would happily explore a relationship with Mike, but I can't. I'm petrified that he'll become collateral damage if Uncle Kelvin ever finds me.

I can't do that to him.

I won't do that to him.

I just can't.

This needs to end before it goes any further. But in doing so, I know that I'm going to break Mike's heart because I know it will break mine too. Breaking his heart is the last thing that I want to do, but it has to be this way.

Mike knocks on the door. "Are you okay, Sav?" I panic that he is going to open it and come in, but he's a gentleman and doesn't open it. I'm frozen, staring at myself in the mirror; I don't know what to say or do. Closing my eyes, I take a deep breath and quietly yell. "Yeah, I'm all good. I'll be out in a minute."

"Okay," he hesitantly replies.

I splash some water on my face, before gabbing my pink, waffle dressing gown. Slipping it on, I take a deep breath and head back into my bedroom to face Mike.

When I open the door, Mike is sitting on the edge of my bed, still naked with the sheet across his lap, I force a smile since he is looking at me. He looks worried and I feel like shit. After what we experienced last night, we should be ecstatically happy, but instead he's dejected and sad. I'm a total chicken and don't ask how he is. I say, "Morning," and offer up a fake smile.

"Morning, babe. You sleep goodly?"

"Like a baby, I was completely worn out."

Smirking, he replies, "Me, too, I haven't slept like that in months."

Reaching his hand out towards me, I step closer to him, but I don't grab his hand, instead I take a seat next to him. Glancing towards him, the sheet has moved and reveals more of his nakedness. I notice that his morning wood has popped out to say hello. Seeing that makes me start to cry...I'll never have his glorious cock inside of me again.

Snapping his head towards me when I start to cry, he whispers, "Sav," as he wraps his arm around me and pulls me into his shoulder. This causes me to cry harder, and I feel like a bitch. He's so sweet and I'm about to break his heart. Glancing up at him, I murmur, "You need to leave, Mike."

"What? Why?"

"I...I...I'm, I just can't do this, Mike," I mumble. "It's not safe." I mustn't mumble the last part quietly enough because Mike lifts my chin so I'm looking directly at him.

"What's not safe, Sav?"

"It's nothing, it's just not safe to be with me. Let's place last night into the 'last-night-was-fucking-amazing-but-can't-happen-again' basket and go back to being friends."

"I don't want that, Sav. I felt something last night, babe, and I know you did, too." He runs his hands over his head, looking back at me. "Where's all this coming from?"

"I'm sorry, Mike, I just can't do this. Last night was beyond amazing but we just can't. I...I just can't." The tears are pouring down my cheeks.

"I call bullshit, Sav, but I'll go and give you space...for now, but don't think I'm giving up on this. I know what I felt last night and I'm not going to let this slide." He stands up, quickly dresses, and before he leaves, he bends down and kisses me on the forehead.

When I hear the front door close, I fall back onto the bed and I cry. My whole body shudders, as the sobs break free. Last night with Mike was out of this world amazing. What I wouldn't give for it to happen again, but I can't. I don't want Mike to get hurt if Uncle Kelvin finds me.

———

The following week is agony. I can't eat. I can't sleep, and work just drags. Mike comes into work every night but I can't look at him. It breaks my heart seeing him; he looks just as sad as I do. As soon as I see him walk in, I find any excuse to be out the back. The stockroom has never been so clean, the boss is impressed and really happy with me; at least that's a positive to come from this.

Jodi notices me take off on Friday night, when Mike comes in, and she corners me out the back, as I'm shoving a handful of Allen's Milk Bottles into my mouth. "Sav, what's going on with you and the hot hulk?"

Giggling at her comment, I say through my mouthful,

"Hot hulk I like that and nothing, absolutely nothing is going on with said hulk."

"Yeah, right, Mole, I'm not stupid. You and he used to flirt up a storm, and I've noticed this week that every time you see him, you come back here. This storeroom has never been this clean or organised, so I know you're hiding from him. Plus he looks like someone ran over his kitty cat."

"Mike hates cats." I pause before quietly adding, "I made a mistake sleeping with him last weekend."

"You slept with him? Fuck, I owe Jude twenty bucks. He said that 's what happened. So do I need to kick his ass for breaking your heart?"

"You bet on me?"

"Yeah, but do I need to kick his ass?" She grabs a handful of Milk Bottles from our secret stash.

"No, you'd need to kick mine."

"What the fuck? Why would you turn him away? He's hotter than hot. Are you crazy?"

"I'm crazy for letting it happen in the first place. Jodi, that night was the best of my life, and now it will never have it again. I'm such a fool." I start to cry again.

Jodi wraps her arms around me. "Shhhh, it's going to be all right, Mole, but why the fuck are you turning him away? The sexual attraction between you two is hotter than Channing Tatum's abs. Blind Freddy can see it, hell even Jude picked it."

"I just can't. There's a part of my life that I don't want to catch up with me, and if it does, I don't want anyone to get caught in the crossfire. If I hook up with

Mike, there's a chance that he'll get hurt. I can't, and most of all, I won't let that happen."

"Shit, what are you running from?"

"It's best you don't know. Please, please don't say anything to anyone. Promise me, Jodi?"

"All right, I promise, but I don't think you should push him away. There is a real spark between you two, and I'd hate for you to miss out on happiness for a what-if."

"Thanks, Jodi, but it's better this way. Let's get back out there before we get in trouble."

We each grab another handful of Milk Bottles and head back out to the bar. Mike is still sitting there and looks up. When he sees me coming towards him, his face lights up; it melts me and only makes this harder. Jodi offers to serve him but I tell her it's fine.

As I'm walking over to Mike, I'm giving myself an internal pep talk. When I reach him, I fake a smile and say, "What can I get you?"

"Hello to you too, Sav. I'll take my usual and another night with you; please."

"Your usual I can do." I pass him his beer and turn to get the tequila. "As for me, sorry that will never happen again." I say this as I slide his tequila across to him, offering a weak smile as he picks it up and sinks his shot.

"Why? Please, at least tell me that?"

"I already told you Mike, I just can't. Please drop it." A tear escapes as I say this, and I quickly wipe it away.

"That's bullshit and you know it, Sav. I'll be here when you're ready to talk."

"You'll be waiting for a long time, Mike."

"I'll wait forever, Sav."

"Mike, no, please don't. Just move on and forget all about me."

"Sav, babe, there is no way in hell I'll be forgetting you, or the other night, anytime soon." He leans over the bar and whispers, "I've tasted your pussy and it's the most delectable pussy I've ever had the pleasure of devouring, and I want more. Your pussy is like crack and I'm addicted. I. Need. More. And, babe, I'm not going anywhere."

Gasping at what he just said, I'm left speechless as he sits back down. He picks up his beer, takes a sip, and smiles at me as if he just said the sky is blue. I stare at him in shock, but I immediately start to remember what his magnificent tongue can do; my undies dampen and I start to smile.

Something by the door catches my eye and my heart immediately stops. Shaking my head, I quickly run over to the door and race outside, but there's no one in sight. Turning around, I walk back inside, this Mike situation is fucking with my head, making me see things. As I'm heading back to the bar, Mike grabs my arm and I jump in fright. "Sav, are you okay? You're as white as a ghost."

"I'm fine, Mike, I just needed some fresh air."

"Yeah right, please talk to me. Maybe I can help?"

Snapping, I yell, "Mike, I'm fine! Just drop it. Please?"

"Fine, but know I'm here for you."

Why the fuck did I sleep with Mike Mustange?

24
———

KELVIN

Look how happy she is, fucking bitch. With all that is hers, she should be living it up somewhere amazing, not living in a shitbox like this. For a fleeting moment, I think that maybe she doesn't know about anything in regards to what I want, but if she doesn't know, why did she run?

I'm camped outside her place, and a baldheaded guy walks up to her door. She seems very happy to see him. Looks like the little slut has a new boyfriend as well. I'm not sure who this guy is, but he stays all day and when he leaves he looks happy...*not for long*, I think to myself, as I head back to the motel.

When I get back to the motel, a wickedly evil plan forms. I laugh out loud; messing with her is going to be ohh so fun. Phase One, texting.

Unknown – *I'll see you soon*

The next morning, I head back to her duplex and

surprise, surprise loverboy is there again; sitting here will be waste of time today, so I head to a local bar to bide my time.

It's just on dusk when I pull up at her place, and I see that dinner has been delivered. From the looks of things, loverboy is still there too. "Damn it!" I shout into the empty car. I was hoping to make a surprise visit tonight, but I don't want any witnesses. I'll wait here until he leaves, then I'll pop in and say good night to my dear old niece.

I've been sitting in my car for over four hours now, and there doesn't seem to be any movement inside, but all the lights are still on. Sneaking over, I quietly climb the front stairs and hear moans and groans coming from her place. That confirms my suspicion that the baldheaded fuck is her boyfriend.

This could be interesting, I think to myself as I'm driving back to the motel. This will change my original plan but it will work out in my favour. As I enter my room, I decide to watch them both for a few days before I make my move.

The next morning, I'm back watching her place bright and early, eventually loverboy leaves. Slamming the door on his way out, I notice that he's really pissed off; naw, shucks, looks like they had a fight. I hope the bitch is miserable.

Taking the chance, I follow him back to his place, so I know where he lives. I'll head back to the little bitch's place later in the morning. It's just before lunchtime when I pull up but she's leaving for work. A night sitting in a bar sounds great to me, I quickly take off and head towards the Black Dungeon. Getting to the pub before her, I head into the corner booth that I have been in for the last week, watching her.

Thanking my lucky stars that she only ever serves from behind the bar, the brunette hottie she works with is extra nice, though. Maybe I can have some fun with her, but she seems to be uptight and won't give me any attention; Jodi is a fucking dick tease bitch; no surprises that her and Savannah would be friends—bitch attracts bitch.

I've noticed the last few nights that whenever loverboy comes in, Savannah ducks and hides out the back, but tonight she serves him at the bar. From here, I can see that there is trouble in paradise. Looks like the using the boyfriend plan is a bust. I've had enough and I'm growing impatient, so I decide to make my presence known tonight...let the games begin.

Looking towards the bar, I see she is talking to ex-loverboy this time. In order to gain her attention, I make a noise, her head snapping towards me. She looks directly at me and I smirk before quickly ducking outside and around the corner, hiding in plain sight.

From my vantage point, I see her come barreling out of the doors, looking around at the empty street. There is fear all over her face and she looks like she is struggling to catch her breath; that makes me so, so happy, I laugh with glee. When she can't see me, or anything in the vicitinty, she heads back inside.

On my way to my car, I laugh and laugh, today was perfect and this tormenting gig is fun. Climbing into my car and I head back to the motel. *Revenge is going to be sweet*, I think as I drive away.

25

MIKE

As usual, I'm at the pub so I can be near Sav. I've turned into a pussy-whipped guy; I'm fucking like Jordan. Even though she is ignoring me, it's nice to be close to her. The afternoon rush is over so I take the chance to talk to Sav. Finally, she is serving me, not hiding, giving me a glimmer of hope. We are talking when all of a sudden she freezes. Her face goes as white as a ghost, her eyes are locked on the front door. She takes off towards the door and heads outside. A feeling of dread washes over me, so I get up to go after her.

Before I reach her, she's already back inside, heading to the bar; reaching out, I grab her elbow. She is shaking like a leaf, and if possible, she is whiter than before. "Are you okay, Sav?" I ask.

"I'm...I'm fine Mike, I just needed fresh air. Just drop it. Please," she begs.

"I call bullshit, Sav. I don't believe you for one second. Please tell me what's going on, maybe I can help?" I'm still gripping her elbow when she pulls free.

Snapping, she yells, "Mike, I'm fine, just drop it!" Pausing, she lowers her voice and pleads with me, her voice wavering, "Please, Mike, *just drop it*." She emphasises the last three words.

"I'm not happy but fine, just know I'm here for you, Sav. Any-fucking-time, day or night." After watching her walk back behind the bar, I sit back down and finish my beer. Sav is avoiding me again and I'm frustrated as all shit. *Women are so confusing*, I think to myself as I finish my beer and head home.

When I get to my place, I grab a bottle of tequila, sit in my favourite easy chair, and catch up on the latest *Bold and the Beautiful* episode, but I can't concentrate. Sav is all I keep thinking about. After the best night of my life, she rejected me and became this different version of Sav: distant, vacant, and aloof.

Last weekend was beyond amazing, and now she wants nothing to do with me. I know I can be an ass at times, but I really thought Sav and I were heading somewhere.

I yell at the TV, "Fuuuuck, why are chicks so confusing?"

Grabbing the bottle of tequila, I sit back and try to come up with a plan to win over Sav, but I just keep getting pissed about the brush off that she gave me. I'm more confused than ever right now. I finish off the bottle of tequila before passing out in my chair watching *RAGE* on *ABC*.

I'm woken early Saturday morning by banging on my front door. Groaning, I slowly get up but hear two little giggles and I smile. Mac and Cheese have come to visit Uncle Mike.

Racing to the door, I open it to find all of the McRoberts clan standing there. My shitty mood instantly disappears and I smile. Reaching out, I grab Indi, *I think*, before saying, in the baby voice that you cannot help but put on when you are around kids, "Hey, gorgeous girl, how's my fav lil' munchkin?"

I head inside with Indi, *I think*, and the rest of them follow me. Kenz sees the empty bottle of tequila on the coffee table and turns to me angrily. "Mike Mustange, why is there an empty bottle of tequila on the coffee table? And now that I look at you, you're tequila hung-over."

Sighing, I sit down and bounce Indi on my knee for a bit, trying to stall. "I'm waiting, Mike Mustange." Looking up I see her standing there with her hand on her hip. Jordan takes a seat next to me and mumbles, "Good luck, dude."

I can't help but laugh and this only pisses Kenz off further. Taking a deep breath I look up at her. "I've had a rough, shitty week, and yesterday after seeing Sav, I couldn't handle it anymore. When I got back here, I just needed to forget and de-stress. I thought a night with Jose was better than going out and screwing around."

"Mike, you've been down this road before, drinking is not the way to deal with things. Now, what happened with Sav?"

"Well, umm, we painted her place last weekend and we had a really nice time. It was fun and then after dinner and a few beers, we slept together."

Looking up, I see both Kenz and Jordan, open-mouthed, staring at me in shock. At the same time, they both speak.

Jordan says, "No fucking way."

While Kenz says, "What did you do to screw it up?"

"Thanks for that vote of confidence, Kenz. She is the one screwing it up. She's pushing me away. I really felt like we had a connection. Now I feel like she used me, and I feel like I'm being sucked back into the 'Mike is a chump' vortex."

"Well," she snaps. Looking at me, she sees how broken up I am, she softly adds. "Have you spoken to her, Mike?"

"I tried last night, Kenz, at the pub. She was working and we were chatting, but then the oddest thing happened and she ran off."

Jordan asks, "What happened?"

"We were talking, well I was, and then she froze, like she saw a ghost and ran outside. When she came back in, she was shaking and whiter than she was before. She told me she was fine and took off back to work. Then she did all she could to avoid me. So I left and came back here to have a party with Jose."

Kenz sits next to me, grabs my hand, and squeezes. "Mike, don't give up on her. I don't know Sav all that well, but I know she's hurting over something. Be the Mike that I know and swoop in and rescue her. You and her are meant to be, Mike, I feel it in my bones."

"I hope you're right, Kenz. I care for her deeply. When we had finished painting, we had a few beers and it felt so good to be with her. We opened up to each other, she told me some pretty personal things. To have her now act like this, I'm totally confused." Looking up at them, I confess, "I really like Sav, guys, like, like her. I haven't felt like this since before the she-devil." Pausing, I smile and add, "Actually, I've never felt like this about anyone."

Both Kenz and Jordan's mouths drop open in shock, and for the first time ever, it seems Kenz is speechless. Not wanting any more attention on Sav and me, I say, "So, what brings the McRoberts gang here today?"

They both are still looking at me in shock, and Kenz is still frozen, when Jordan says, "Well, we are taking the girls to the beach, and we thought we'd stop and see if Unky Mike wants to come, too?"

"A day at the beach sounds awesome. Kenz, you got any brownies?" I think to myself, *I would love for Sav to join us, maybe another time...I hope.*

"Not today, sorry, dude, but I did try a new choc chip peanut butter cookie recipe. Jordan has already eaten half of them, so I guess they must be okay."

Smiling, Jordan adds, "Dude, they are no brownie, but they are still pretty amazeballs. There is not much that my wonderful, hot, sexy, awesome wife can't do."

Raising my hand, I smart-assly add, "She can't walk without tripping over, but her cooking skills certainly make up for her unco-ness."

"Fuck off, Mike!" she defensively says, while giving me the finger.

Jordan scolds her, "Kenz, babe, settle down, he was only joking. What's up with your emotions at the moment?"

"I don't know." Sheepishly, she looks over at me. "Sorry, Mike. I didn't mean to snap like that."

"It's all good, babe. But can I say, that was hot seeing you get all feisty like that."

Shaking her head, smiling, she says, "You are totally weird. Now, go get changed, so we can head to the beach, before it gets too hot."

Getting up, I head down the hall and I hear Kenz say to Jordan, "I'm going to get Mike and Sav together, you didn't see them that night at the Dungeon."

Jordan whisper-shouts. "Stay out of it, Kenz."

As I'm changing into my boardies and singlet, I decide that I'm going to win Sav's heart, and I will do whatever it takes; including getting Kenz to help me if needed.

But first, I need to get to the bottom of her pulling away.

26

SAV

MY LIFE HERE WAS GOING SO WELL AND THEN stupidly, or amazingly, depending on how you look at it, I let go last night. Now it's all falling apart, why-o-why did I sleep with Mike Mustange?

I'll tell you why, he's a baldheaded, six-foot demigod, with a heart of gold. I was thinking with my vagina, rather than my head, that's why, stupid vagina. But it can't go any further, what if Uncle Kelvin finds me? I can't have him being collateral damage, I just can't.

It's moments like this that I really wish Jace was still here. He'd know exactly what to say and do. He'd tell me to pull my head out of my ass and go for it with Mike, because Mike is a good guy, and I deserve to be happy too.

What if Uncle Kelvin finds me?

What if Mike's in an accident?

I can't lose another person that I love, yes love. I am in love with Mike Mustange after one amazing night.

I just can't risk it!

While I'm sitting here contemplating what I'm going to do, there's a knock at the door. I freeze. What if it's Mike, back to confront me after this morning? When I hear them yell, "Hello, anyone home? I have a delivery for a Ms. Savannah Blac."

Sighing in relief, I get up and shout, "Coming," as I head to the door. Swinging the door open, there's a young delivery dude with a huuuuuuge bunch of lilies and ginormous box with a silver bow.

"Hi, are you Savannah?"

"Yep, that's me. Who's it from?" I ask excitedly. I've never received anything like this before.

"No idea, sorry. I'm just the delivery guy, where do you want me to put these and this?"

"Umm, on the table will be great."

He shuffles past me and puts the flowers and package on the table. Turning, he asks me to sign the clipboard that was sitting on top of the box. I sign and he leaves, closing the door behind him.

When I realise the flowers are lilies, I smile; lilies were Mum's favourite and they smell heavenly. Opening the box, I see that there is a six-pack of *Schofferhoffer* and a tub of *Skittles*. Standing there staring at the box, a strange feeling washes over me when I realise there's no card, which I find odd. *Why would I receive an anonymous package that has Mum, Dad, and Jace's fav things in it?* That strange feeling intensifies as I put the flowers in some water.

I don't need this right now; my life is confusing enough. I decide to have a bath, maybe it will relax me, and I will see things more clearly. The candles are lit, the wine is chilling, and the water is the perfect temperature. My iPod is charged and currently Everclear is singing about a heroin girl, and the bath bubbles are bubbly and smell divine. I submerge myself and try to relax, but I can't.

I can't stop thinking about Mike Mustange.

Every time I close my eyes, my mind drifts back and I see his head between my legs. Vividly, I remember the intoxicating feeling that overtook my body as his tongue lavished me and his hands massaged my breasts.

Taking a sip of wine, I close my eyes and try to relax, but once again Mike appears. With my eyes still closed, my fingers drift down my chest and over my nipples; twisting and pulling as they snake their way down to my pulsating pussy. I rub my clit in circles before slipping a finger inside. I place my wine glass on the ledge behind me and pull on my nipple with my free hand. My fingers continue to thrust in and out. I moan, "Mike!" as my orgasm hits and I slosh water all over the bathroom.

Opening my eyes, I see water splashed everywhere but I don't care. My body is still tingling from the most intense self-induced orgasm I've ever had. *I'm so screwed*, I think to myself as I climb out of the bath. Drying off, I change into my sleep shorts and singlet before mopping up the mess that I made.

Climbing into my bed, I smile. It still smells like Mike and I drift off to sleep, once again, thinking about Mike Mustange.

———

This week is going extremely slow and my mind is all over the place. I keep stuffing up orders, dropping things, and turning up late or early. Mike is constantly on my mind. He has been into the Dungeon every shift, and I've tried my hardest to avoid him. For the most part, I have succeeded, but it's getting harder and harder to stay away from him. I have to remain strong.

On Wednesday, I received another bunch of lilies and once again, no note. This is really starting to freak me out, I wish I had someone to talk to, but I'm better off being alone. I don't want anyone to get hurt because of me.

It's now Saturday night and the Dungeon is packed. I'm rushed off my feet as Jodi, the bitch, called in sick. Understaffed, plus Saturday night equals bedlam at the best of times. Mike is here, again, and tonight is the night that he finally confronts me about last night. We didn't really get a chance to chance to talk properly after I thought I saw Uncle Kelvin, but thankfully, it gets busy and can again brush him and his inquisition off...for now anyway.

I'm not one-hundred-percent sure, but I'm pretty certain it was him. The uncertainty is what is freaking me out. I deduce that it wasn't him because if it were, he'd confront me; there is no way he'd hang back. He wants this more than life itself, so if he found me, I'd know about it.

On my way home after the shift from hell, I think about everything going on: mystery packages, Mike, Uncle Kelvin; what the hell am I going to do?

I'M SITTING IN MY FLEA-INFESTED MOTEL ROOM, drinking a can of *Emu* beer, and I can't help but laugh. My surprise package should be delivered to the little bitch, right about now. It cost me a fucking fortune to send all the shit to her, but taunting her is going to be so much fun. Laughing as I get up to grab another beer, I think about her reaction. I so wish I could be there to see her face when she gets it.

It gives me ideas on sending other packages, but I don't want to waste too much money, or time, on this. This investigator already cost me a fucking fortune. *Thank fuck he came through though*, I think to myself as I grab another beer.

___

A few days later, I decide that I need to get out of this shithole. As I'm putting my shoes on, I decide to swing by the bitch's house and see if she got my latest surprise, but she's not home. It's late afternoon so I guess that she will be at work. My throat is a little dry, so I decide to head to the bar and see the little whore.

Seeing the shock on her face when I popped into her line of sight last week was priceless. I can't wait until I confront her face-to-face. This toying with her is so much fun, until I get what's rightfully mine, I'm going to play.

I've decide to up my game. I'm now sending daily anonymous notes to her. I've been leaving them at her duplex, on her car, and at her work; luckily she works with idiots and they are happy to take the notes whenever I drop by.

After dropping a note off at her place, I have to get out of there quickly as her friend with the kids turns up. I was hoping to see her face when she got this one, but I guess, it will have to wait for another time.

As I'm driving away, I remember how scared she was after the last attack, so I decide that another attack is in order. After I arrange it; I get a good feeling, this will be it. Soon, I will finally get what is mine.

I'm hiding out at home because I'm too gutless to face Mike, or anyone, for that matter. It's fine, I have my books, tequila, and wine so all is goodly. I'm staring at the walls that Mike and I painted and become sad. I miss spending time with him, but I can't get close to him. I'd never forgive myself if Uncle Kelvin did anything to him. I'm now convinced it was him that I saw the other night, and I won't risk Mike getting hurt, he's too nice for that.

Sighing, I get up and think that it's WTF–Wine Time Finally–when there is a knock at the door. Pausing midstep, I try to pretend I'm not here but they knock again. I stay frozen on the spot, then I hear, "Open up Sav, it's Kenz. I know you're home." Pausing she adds, "I have wine."

Laughing, I turn and head towards the door. Swinging it open, I see Kenz's sparkling green eyes and a super big smile, her cheeriness and smile are infectious, and I find myself beaming back at her.

"Hey, lady, I thought it was time we hung out, it's been far too long."

"It sure has, Kenz, it sure has. Come on in."

Turning, I see a piece of paper poking out from under the front doormat. I bend down and pick it up as Kenz shuffles past me. I open the piece of paper and freeze. My hands start to shake and I gasp. Kenz spins around and looks worried.

"Are you okay, Sav?"

"Umm, yeah, it's all good, but I just remembered that I have an appointment to get to. Can we do wine another time?"

"Yeah, sure that's fine." She walks towards me and reaches out to rub my arm. "Are you sure you're okay, Sav? You're as white as a ghost."

"Yeah, nah, I'm fine. Just tired. I did close last night and didn't sleep very well when I got home."

Kenz hands me the wine. "Here, you keep this here for our catch up. By the way, the lounge room looks great. You and Mike did a really good job."

"Yeah, it came up so much better than I imagined. Mike's pretty awesome."

Smirking at what I said, Kenz says, "He sure is awesome. We will catch up soon." She squeezes my arm and heads out. Closing the door behind her, I lock it before sinking to the floor, wrapping my arms around my knees, hugging them to my chest, and I cry.

A few hours later, I'm still sitting in the same spot by the front door. My eyes are swollen from crying, my face is all mascara stained, *so much for waterproof,* and I'm stiff from not moving for a long time. All of a sudden, there is a thump at the front door; I startle with fright. As I stand to open the door, the hairs on the back of my neck prickle. I unlock the door, and I'm just about to turn the handle, when it's shoved open, and I fall back on my ass with a thud.

Looking up, I see a masked man standing over me; before I have time to move, he kicks me in the stomach. The pain is nothing like I've felt before; I curl into a ball to protect myself. He grabs my shoulders and pushes me flat, straddling my chest. Lifting his palm, he slaps me hard across the face and roughly grabs my chin. My face is tingling and I see stars from the shock and force of the slap, I begin to cry.

He gets right up in my face and spits, "This is just a warning, give him what he wants and you will never see me again. You don't want to see what I'm capable of." He slaps me again before standing up, looming over at me; he glares. "Remember my warning, bitch." He steps over me and kicks me in the hard in ribs again before walking out, slamming the door behind him.

Lying on the floor in agony, I continue to cry. My ribs are aching, it hurts to breathe, and my face is still tingling. The sobs overtake my body, and with each breath, it gets harder and harder to breathe; eventually I pass out from the pain.

It's the middle of the night when I wake up; the room is dark except for the streetlight shining through the front window. I'm still on the floor in the lounge room, but this time I'm numb; I cannot feel anything. I'm staring at the ceiling, feeling defeated when I realise I need to pee. Rolling to my side, I try to sit up, but I struggle. Every time I move, my ribs throb; at least my face has stopped tingling and it's less painful to breathe now.

Finally, I manage to stand up. The room starts to spin, so I stand on the spot, waiting for it to pass. Holding onto the door for support, I wait for the dizziness to pass. As soon as I feel okay, I slowly make my way to the bathroom. I go to the toilet and then wash my hands. Looking up, I see my reflection staring back and I don't recognise the girl I see.

She's broken.

Alone.

Ready to give up.

The tears start to fall again; I don't know what to do.

———

The night after my attack, someone knocking at my door wakes me; I recognise the knock as Mike's. It makes me smile but also sad at the same time. I lay here hoping that he will eventually go away, but he's a persistent bastard and keeps knocking. Groaning, I ease out of bed, cringing at my rib pain and yell, "Be there in a minute, Mike!"

He shouts back, "How did you know it was me?"

Smiling as I walk down the hallway, I hurry to the door. Opening it with a big smile on my face, I huskily say, "I know your knock. It's as unique as you, Mike Mustange." I wink and smirk, placing my hand on my hip.

He smiles back at me and then his face drops, "Holy shit! What happened to your face, Sav?"

Shit...fuck...shit, how am I going to get out of this? I

think to myself. Deciding to go with a half-truth, I reply shyly, "Some asshole tried to mug me when I was coming home. He hit me, but I kicked him in the balls and he ran off."

"Fuck, Sav, why didn't you call me? I would have come and helped you."

"As you can see, Mike, I'm fine. Nothing to worry about. I was just about to make coffee, you want to come in?"

Turning to the settee on my verandah, he picks up a tray of coffee and a Java Lava paper bag. My tummy rumbles at just that moment, and we both laugh. He says, "Guess you're happy I'm here then?"

Without evening thinking, I reply. "I'm always happy to see you, Mike. Now, give me my coffee, asshole."

"Wow, you're just as much of a grump bum in the morning before coffee as Kenz is."

Laughing, he passes me a coffee as we both head inside to the couch. I wince as we sit, but I don't think Mike noticed, he and his banana bread are having a moment and I smile. "Should I leave you and your banana bread here alone?"

Midbite, he smugly replies, "If you don't mind, that'd be great."

Shaking my head, I just laugh at him. We sit here in silence and enjoy our coffees. Glancing over at him, I wish things could be different, but I now know that after last night's visit; there can never be a Mike and Sav. Mike looks up and sees me checking him out and he winks at me. Ovaries: BOOM.

Mike and I chat for about an hour, we have inched

ourselves closer to each other, and he starts to rub circles on my thigh. It stirs my insides. I glance over and see him staring intently at me. Without even thinking, I lean over and kiss him.

His lips are softer than I remember, I moan as I slip my tongue into his mouth. Our tongues caressing, hands wandering over each other, he tweaks my nipples through my singlet and I run my hands over his smooth head. Wrapping my arms around his neck, I straddle his hips and deepen our kiss.

He groans as I rub myself on his growing erection. He wraps his arms around me, squeezing me tight, crushing my ribs and I flinch in pain. That's enough to bring me back to earth and I quickly jump off Mike. Looking down at him, I feel like a total bitch when I say, "I'm sorry, Mike, I...I shouldn't have done that. I...I think you need to leave."

He doesn't move a muscle; he sits there staring up at me. His eyes boring into my soul, I'm so close to saying fuck it when Mike stands up. He gets right up into my face and says, "Sav, you can keep pushing me away and I will keep pushing back. I feel something here and I know you do, too. I'm not going anywhere, babe, so you better get used to it." I go to interrupt him but he places his finger over my lips. "I'm not finished. I know you are hiding something and that something is big. But I want you to know, I'm here when you're ready to talk."

He gently brushes a tendril of my blonde hair behind my ear; his touch makes my body tingle from head to toe. He leans closer to me. I can feel his breath on my neck; it's warm and smells like coffee. Closing my eyes, I sigh when he quietly and seductively whispers in my ear, "I'm...NOT...going...anywhere, Sav." Bending down, he kisses my cheek, before turning around and leaving. He quietly closes the door behind him as he goes.

I'm left standing there, by my couch, in shock, panting and completely turned on. I really want to chase after him but I know I can't. I'm now even more confused than before...if that's possible.

The next week passes by in a blur. It's a continual cycle of work, sleep, avoid everyone; and repeat. Mike has sent me a text daily to see how I am; I reply with, "yep, all good" **inserting a smiley face or emoji**. He also sends me random funny GIFs; they always make me laugh.

Kenz has blown my phone up with texts, missed calls, and voicemails. I'm horrible and haven't replied to her, well that was until I received a text from Jordan, pleading with me to reply to Kenz. Apparently, she is driving him nuts. I messaged her, apologising about being busy and not getting back to her sooner. She seems to buy it when we make arrangements to catch up next week.

I'm dreading going into work tonight, I'm just not in the mood but I'm on with Jodi. She owes me an explanation for flaking the other week, not that I can be too mad because I have been all over the place the last few weeks. She has become a great friend and always manages to puts a smile on my face, so I'm sure it will be a good shift...if only I knew what would happen.

29

MIKE

I'M REALLY WORRIED ABOUT SAV, ESPECIALLY AFTER her mugging. I'm so pissed she didn't call me to help her. Ever since, she hasn't been herself and it's not just because she's avoiding me. Normally she has the biggest smile on her face, and when she enters a room, the atmosphere immediately brightens. But lately, she seems so sad, broken, and despondent; not that happy Sav that we all love.

Each time I have seen her this week, I've tried to get her to open up, but she's shutting me out. She's been shutting everyone out, at least it's not just me. It seems all that she does at the moment is work and sleep. She never goes anywhere—yes, that sounds stalkerish, but I'm really worried about her.

I'm over at Kenz and Jordan's, and Kenz and I are chatting while we wait for Jordan to get home. I'm cuddling and playing with Indi and Rory - I still can't tell the munchkins apart, but they are so cute that thankfully cutie pie or munchkin works. We get onto the topic of Sav. "Mike, what's up with Sav?"

"What do you mean, Kenz?"

"Something is off, she doesn't seem herself at the moment. The other day, I went over to her place to catch up and have a wine. She picked up a note that was tucked under the doormat, and when she read it, her face went white and she made up some excuse about forgetting an appointment. She told me we would have to catch up another time. Whatever was in that note really freaked her out."

"She never mentioned anything about a note to me, but yeah; I have noticed that she's not herself. She was mugged about a week ago, so maybe she's just freaked out from that."

"Shit, that sucks ass. Why didn't she tell anyone?"

"Beats me, Kenz. We have kinda been on the outs since we slept together, and it hasn't gotten any better. But she seems different and not herself, that's for sure. " Pausing, I look over at her and add, "I really like her, Kenz. I know I said after De-Niece that I wasn't going there again, but I can't stop thinking about her. Her pushing me away has really fucked with my head. Maybe it's better if I just leave it be. Kenz, what if she's like De-Niece?"

She punches me in the arm, really hard. For a little chick, she has a wicked right hook. "Mike, you're an asshat."

"Why am I an asshat?"

"Oh My God! Mike Mustange, you are a total douchcanoe asshole if you think that about her. Sav is nothing, NOTHING, like that crazy, psycho bitch Barbie." She pauses then adds, "May she burn in hell for all eternity with her equally psycho cousin."

"Tell us how you really feel, Kenz. But I get it; I'm just freaked out. I told myself I was never going there again and when I do open up, it punches me in the junk." I look over to Kenz and smile. "But there is something about Sav. I haven't been able to get her off my mind since she started at the Dungeon. I find myself there most days, and if I don't see her, I get sad. When I do see her, my heart warms and I get all tingly and shit. Fuck, I'm turning into Jordan, I'm becoming a pussy."

"No, Mike, it just means you've met someone special, maybe even 'the one.' Your reactions are normal, Mike. You've never felt this before, and it's making your man bits all giddy, and your teeny tiny little brain doesn't know how to react to that."

"My man bits don't get giddy, thank you very muchly."

"Whatevs, Mike. All I'm saying is that you really like Sav and that's why you are freaking out. And you want to know a secret?"

"It's you, Kenz, you're gonna tell me regardless of what I say. So spill."

"I think she likes you too, but she's scared for some reason."

Snapping my head up, I look at Kenz. "Then why did she fuck and chuck?"

"I don't know, Mike, but you need to find out. Now,

go and see what's up with our girl. I need another girl-friend and I kinda like this one."

"But you have Sarah."

"Something is up with her. She's doing a Sav and pulling away from me. I ran into Josh the other day, apparently they broke up."

"What the fuck?"

"Tell me about it. That was the first I heard, too."

"What did Sarah say when you spoke to her?"

"She's been avoiding me, BUT I guess if she and Josh have just split, then that would be why. I know what she's like. I'll give her space until she's ready...or until I can't stand it anymore, and I'll pin her down 'til she talks."

"Okay, well let me know if she needs anything. Can I ask a fav, Kenz?"

"Of course, Mike. What do you need?"

"Do you think I could steal Jordan for a guys' night tonight?"

"Of course, but on one condition."

"I'm kinda scared right now, before I agree, what's your condition?"

"Next weekend, can you watch the girls? I wanna take my man out for a night. It's been forever since he and I have had any one-on-one time."

"Ummm, if you have them in bed, and I don't have to change a shitty ass, I can do it."

"I can help with the sleeping part but I have no control of their bowels." She sweetly smiles at me.

"Fine, I'll do it. Lucky I love you, Kenz."

The front door opens, just as I say that and Jordan walks in. "Dude, why the fuck are you loving my wife...

again?" He bends down and places a kiss on Indi's head before heading over to Kenz and Rory.

"Your wonderful wife is letting you off your chain tonight, and we are going to the Dungeon, guys' night. Then I'm on daddy duty next weekend, so you and your hot mumma can get your jiggy on."

Kenz shakes her head, and says. "And by 'get our jiggy on' he means dinner and a few cocktails."

I burst our laughing, "Kenz, darlin', you and 'few' don't go together...ever." I air quote few.

"Fuck off, Mike, I do so know how to handle myself. I'm a mum now and I'm totally responsible."

Jordan and I both start laughing. "Just like you were responsible the night I let you and him loose at the Dungeon, a few weeks ago. If I remember correctly, you fertilised the front garden, the verandah, and the bed."

"I blame Mike."

"Hey, don't blame me, lady. I told you Jose wasn't a good choice. But yeah, we totally had a great night, up until I got you home that is."

"Dude, you dropped her off and took off quicker than a fat kid inhaling a bucket of KFC. I had to deal with her drunk ass and look after Indi and Rory...for the next two days."

I'm in stitches listening to this. "Fuck, I love you guys. All right, asshat, the master has given you the night off. Go get changed and we will head to the Dungeon for a night of funness."

"Who died and made you boss?"

"Dude, I've always been the boss. You just haven't realised until now. Now go, I need to get my drink on."

Jordan looks towards Kenz. "Are you sure, babe?"

"Yep, all good. Mike helped me with the girls and I'm about to put them down. Fingers crossed they sleep through like they did last night. Ever since Mike said it, I've been looking forward to a quiet night. It's gonna be me, wine, Jerry, and Striker."

I look at her confused. "What flavour Jerry? And who the fuck is Striker?"

"Duh, Choc Chip Cookie Dough, and Striker is the hero in the book I'm currently reading. It's a book that Sarah recommended. Actually, Mike, you'd really like this one."

"Sweet, send me the link and I'll one-click when I get home."

"You are such a fucking girl, Mike. Grab a beer, I'll help Kenz get the girls down and then we can go."

"And you love me and my girlyness. Hey, do you have any of the beer?"

"And which beer would that be?"

"The new one that I really like."

"Nah, not at home. It's only at Malt Me. We could go there tonight, if you want to?"

I panic when he says this because I really want to see Sav. "Nah, it's all good. You probably don't want to go back to work; we can go to the Dungeon. They have these amazing wings at the moment. I think you'll like them."

"Yeah, we are going there for the wings and not some hot, blonde bar bitch." *Fucker*, I think to myself. "Now pass me my princess so we can get our drink on."

I hand Indi to him and whisper, "She's not a bitch," before heading to the kitchen to grab a beer. While I'm waiting, I download that book onto my phone that Kenz mentioned, and I start to read while I wait. She's right, as usual; *Fractured Affections* is great. It's different and this Striker dude is awesome, just like me, and Reagan is a total MILF.

Tonight is going to be epic; I can feel it now.

30

MIKE

JORDAN AND I ARE IN A CAB ON OUR WAY TO THE Dungeon, and I start to get nervous when we pull up. I'm really looking forward to seeing Sav tonight, but I'm also apprehensive at the same time. I start to panic a little when I realise that there is a chance she won't be working. We walk inside and my eyes immediately scoot around the room looking for her. Glancing towards the bar, I see a sexy ass up on a ladder; two perfect buns encased in dark denim; I recognise that ass. My eyes roam up higher, and low and behold, it's Sav.

Smiling, Jordan and I head towards the bar. I adjust my dick but it's getting harder and harder, literally, as we get near. Up close her ass is just perfect, I totally want to bite that butt and sink myself balls deep into her tight hole. She totally looks absolutely stunning tonight.

She spies Jordan and me. I'm totally caught checking her out, and she nearly falls of the ladder when I wink at her. She carefully climbs down and walks over to us, just as the other bartender comes to take our order. She reaches out and grabs his arm, I'm jealous of the hold she has on him. "I got these two, Randy. Can you swap the Heni keg over, please? It just ran out." He nods and heads out back to change the keg over.

She smiles at us. "Hey, guys, what can I get ya?"

Jordan takes a seat and I stand, my cock is still at half-mast and I need him to go down before I can sit comfortably. *Think of Grandpa and Grandma doing it,* I keep saying to myself. "Hey, Sav. Mike and I will have his usual, thanks."

She looks at Jordan apprehensively. "Jordan, you want a beer with a tequila chaser? I thought you and tequila go together like oil and water?"

I start to laugh. "No tequila for pussy boy, he'll take a black sambuca." I slap him on the back before looking back at Sav. "Hi, by the way." I feel like a bloody teenager, I'm so nervous around her tonight. My heart is racing, my palms are sweaty, and every time I look at her, my cocks twitches.

It's pretty full at the Dungeon tonight and tables are sparse, so Jordan and I decide to hang at the bar. Not that I'm complaining because it means I'm closer to Sav.

Sitting at the bar with Jordan reminds me of our college days and of a less confusing time in my life. "Dude, this reminds me of our college days."

"Yeah, it kinda does hey. What was the name of that bar we used to go to?"

"Umm, it's right on the tip of my tongue." I pause as I try and think, "Yep, I got nothing. Total mind blank."

"Naw, is your little brain struggling to remember?"

"Fuck off, asshat, you tell me the name then, Mr. I-Can-Remember?"

"Yeah, nah, I'm drawing a blank. How about we make a wager, person to remember first wins. Loser paying for tonight's drinks?"

"You're on, dude, prepare to lose."

We both spit and shake on it, just as Sav comes over. "Oh My God, you two are bloody gross." We both just shrug our shoulders at her.

"Yep." Jordan and I say in unison.

"Ugh, just wash your hands before you touch anything." Shaking her head at us. She add, "Can I get you boys another round?"

"That would be awesome, Sav. You sure you don't want to work at Malt Me? We could do with someone like you there."

"Thanks, but I'm happy here, Jordan. I'll get your drinks and be right back."

Just as Sav is sliding the shots across the bar, I shout, "Dirty Duck!"

"Fuuuuck, I lost...again." Jordan complains.

"Dude, you should know better than to bet against me. You think you'd learn after all these years."

"Fuck off, asshole, you can drink lime and soda for the rest of the night."

"Get fucked, asshat. Don't be a sore loser."

Jordan and I are having a great night and it is just what I needed...if only I knew what was around the corner.

31

KELVIN

TONIGHT IS THE NIGHT THAT I'M GOING TO LET THE little bitch know that I've found her, and I won't be leaving until she knows that I mean business; no more Mister Nice Kelvin. The attack was a bust, I was hoping that the thug I hired this time would have scared her shitless, but she seems to have grown a backbone since moving here. She just went about her everyday life as if nothing happened; that was a waste of fucking money.

The aces I hold up my sleeve, to get her to cave, are loverboy and her mummy friend. *This could get interesting and I like it*, I think to myself as I finish off another *Fosters*.

From my research, I know that she will be working this evening so looks like I'm off to the pub for the evening; at least the bitch works at a pub and this can be extra fun. I arrive before her shift starts so that I have more of a chance to hide myself. I want my reveal to be spectacular. I don't want the little bitch to see it coming.

Her bootylicious, bar bitch friend, Jodi, is working

tonight, and I flirt up a storm with her each time she comes by my booth. What I wouldn't give to pound my cock into her, but I have other things to tend to first. A night with her can be my reward once I get what's mine.

Looking towards the bar I see loverboy and his friend take a seat at there. The sexual attraction between her and him is electric, but there's tension that's as thick as my cock. You could cut through it with a knife...the tension, not my cock.

Finally, I see Savannah go towards the bathrooms and head out back; it's now or never. Getting up from the table, I head towards where she went, my heart rate increases as I realise I'm about to get what's mine. *It's show time*, I think to myself as I walk across the bar.

Sneaking up behind her, I tap her on the shoulder. She jumps before spinning around. When she realises it's me behind her; the look on her face is priceless, and she's frozen on the spot. I seriously wish I had a camera right now. "Why, hello, niece."

"Wh...what are you doing here?" she stutters.

"I've come to get what's mine and I know you know what it is. This dumb, sweet, innocent act ends tonight." Pausing, I grip her upper arm tightly and between clenched teeth I spit, "I want it now!"

Pleading, she whines, "I have no idea what you want, Uncle Kelvin."

She is pissing me off with the innocent bullshit, so I slap her hard across the face, the crack echoing down the dark hallway. "Don't fuck with me, bitch." She's holding her cheek and begins to cry. "Your tears won't work on me. The solution is simple, Savannah, give me what I want, and then I'll leave you alone."

"Fine, I'll sign the stores over to you."

I laugh, a deep belly laugh, "You really are a dumb bitch. I don't want the stores. I want what your mother, father, and grandparents kept from me. You don't want to end up with the same fate as them, do you?"

She's staring up at me in shock. I don't think what I just let slip has actually registered yet. Roughly, I bend down and squeeze her upper arms again and begin violently shaking her from side to side, her head lolling about as I shove her out the back door and into the alley. "I will give you a week to give me what's mine, Savannah, otherwise I can't guarantee the safety of loverboy." Pausing for effect, I stare directly into her eyes and I sneer, "Or your hot mummy friend and her babies."

"No, please don't hurt them, Uncle Kelvin. Please?" Her begging is quite pathetic.

Slapping her across the cheek again, I get right up in her face and I spit, "Don't fuck with me, bitch, I want what's mine. You have one week."

Spinning around, I walk back towards to door I just came through, turning before I warn, "And don't even think about contacting the police, that will just make things much more dreadful...for them, anyway."

Opening the door, I step through, before closing it, I look back at her, quivering and shaking in the alley. Laughing, I declare, "And, Savannah, don't disappoint me." With that final remark, I slam the door and leave the bar, laughing on my way out.

32

MIKE

Jordan has just left to head home but I decide to stay on, hoping to chat to Sav, as I haven't spoken to her in a few days. To be honest, I'm worried about her. She seems so sad, so vulnerable, even frightened at the moment. I want the happy, always smiling, makes me laugh, sends blood rushing to my cock, Sav back. Well, she still stirs my cock; she's always sexy, just sad and aloof.

Heading out the back for some fresh air, I take a deep breath when I hear crying coming from behind the industrial bins. I cautiously make my way over and crouching down, I see it's Sav. She lifts her head up, her cheeks streaked with black from her mascara, as the tears cascade down her beautiful cheeks. She looks broken and fragile, but most of all terrified. Taking a deep breath, with sad eyes, she whispers, "Please, help me."

Racing over to her, I bend down and pull her into a hug. For the first time in weeks, she doesn't pull away; she wraps her arms around my waist and continues to cry.

Her cries increase into full-blown sobs, her tears wetting my shirt but I don't care. All I care about is making Sav feel better. I hold Sav in my arms for what feels like hours, but in actual fact it's only a few minutes.

She pulls back and looks up at me and smiles; her expression melts my heart. But her smile doesn't last long, her eyes frantically dart around the alley. All I can now see in her eyes in fear. "Sav, babe, what's wrong?"

"Ummm...I'm just having a rough night."

I scoff, "Rough night my ass. When I came out here you were beside yourself and you said 'please help me' when I approached you."

"Nnn...no I didn't. I said please leave me alone."

"Sav, don't lie to me."

She hangs her head and starts to cry again. After a few moments, she lifts her head and looks up at me. "I...I can't do this again. I thought I got away. I've got to get out of here." She tries to get out of my arms but I hold her tighter.

"Let me help you, Sav."

"No, I...I have to go."

Sav manages to get free and runs off. I'm standing there in the alley watching her run back inside the bar. *She may have gotten away from me, but I will help her, whether she wants me to or not.*

33

SAV

WHEN I FINALLY GET HOME AFTER MY SHIFT, I FIND Mike sitting on my doorstep. I pause midstep. "What are you doing here?"

He looks up at me; I see lust and confusion in his eyes. "I just wanted to make sure you were okay."

"Well, as you can see, I'm fine. You can leave now."

"Sav, babe, I'm not going anywhere until you tell me the truth."

"Mike, I'm fine. There's nothing to tell."

"You are not fine, Sav, don't bullshit a bullshitter. Now, I'm going to ask you one more time, what's wrong?"

"I...I...I'm not fine but I don't want to drag you into my problems, Mike. They are mine and mine alone."

"Sav, I'm not going anywhere until you tell me. If you like, I can call Kenz, and we both know what she's like. She won't let it go until she knows what's going on. It's your call, me or Kenz."

My heads snaps up, I believe that he would do that and Kenz is relentless when she wants to know something. Sighing, I look up at Mike and smile shyly. "Fine, come inside. I'll tell you, but you have to promise to not tell Kenz...or anyone, for that matter."

He crosses his heart and says, "Cross my heart, hope to die. Stick a needle in my cock."

Laughing, I shake my head and give up in defeat. "Fine, come on in and I'll tell you." Walking past Mike, I unlock the door, flick on the light switch, and walk inside. "Take a seat, I'll be right back."

To stall and wrap my head around the events from tonight, I head into my bedroom and change. Sighing in relief as I take my bra off, I hate wearing that thing, before slipping on a pair of denim shorts and a black singlet. After changing, I head back out, taking a deep breath I give myself an internal pep talk. *You tell him, he freaks, he leaves and then I can plan my escape*, all good. Repeating this over and over as I head down the hall towards Mike and the lounge room.

Halfway down the hall, I decided that this conversation needs tequila, so I stop and grab a bottle of Patrón, two shot glasses, and two beers before heading toward Mike.

Pausing midstride, I see Mike sitting on my couch; he is so ruggedly sexy; *I wish things could be different*, I think to myself. My girly bits start throbbing and I imagine him pinning me to the couch as he ravishes my body...again. He looks up and smiles at me, it shoots straight to my girly bits and my undies dampen. The throbbing between my thighs increases the closer I get to Mike. I shake my head; I can't be thinking of this right now, I have much bigger things going on. "This conversation needs tequila. I know you like tequila, so I didn't think you'd mind. I grabbed some beers as well."

"Wow, I'm kind of scared of this conversation if both tequila and beer are needed." Pausing, his eyes roam over my body, stopping at my tits before he looks me I the eyes. "Sav, I'm not going anywhere until I get the truth, so take a seat and tequila me up, baby."

Laughing, I sit next to Mike and pour us each a shot; I down mine and pour another. Passing Mike his shot, our fingers touch and I feel an electric spark between us. I know he feels it, too. He's staring intently at me, his eyes ablaze with lust; a reflection of what mine currently look like.

My breathing becomes shallow as we keep staring at each other. Breaking the connection, I look towards the window, staring at the curtains. *I can't be falling for Mike.* There is too much at stake, especially now that Uncle Kelvin has found me and I finally know what he is after. I can't and won't let him hurt Mike, or Kenz and the babies...or me.

Looking back up, I see Mike starting intently at me. "I'm waiting, Sav."

"I know, I'm just trying to decide where to start."

"The beginning is usually a good place."

"Fuck you, Mike," I snap, "This isn't easy for me. I thought I'd gotten away and now...now it's all gone to shit 'cause he found me."

"Who found you?"

"My uncle."

"What do you mean he found you?"

"It's all going to start again." The tears started to flow,

"I can't do this for a second time, I barely survived the first." Mike reaches over and wraps his arms around me. I relax into him, it feels so good to be in his embrace, and now I'm even more conflicted.

He pulls back and looks into my eyes. "I'm confused, Sav, which is easy I know, but I thought you said you didn't have any family left after the accident?"

"I did and I don't. He's not my family, we may share the same bloodline, but that's it. He lost the right to be called family when he had those thugs attack me."

"What the fuck?"

"I'm gonna need another shot before I start." We both have a shot and I take a sip of my beer. "As I said a few weeks back, my world came crashing down eight months ago when I lost Mum, Dad, and Jace. What I didn't tell you is that after the will reading my uncle turned nasty. He'd come over blind, rotten drunk most nights and he'd ransack the house, looking for something. He'd always rant that I was hiding it from him, just like my parents; that I was a selfish bitch and so on. He himself never hit me but the verbal abuse was just as bad. One night, four people came to the house. They ransacked the place pretty bad, looking for it and...and one of them physically assaulted me." The tears start to flow again, taking a deep breath I add, "I ended up in hospital for a few days. I know he hired them to scare me, or for them to find what he's been looking, for but I had no proof." Taking another gulp of beer, I continue, "It was while I was in hospital that I decided I was going to leave. I made arrangements to sell the house, closed up everything, and here I am."

"Fuck me, what as ass. He's your uncle. He's your family."

"You're telling me. I also lied, Mike. I wasn't mugged last week. Someone came here and attacked me." Pausing, I look over at him. "I'm pretty sure he was behind the attack, too."

"Are you fucking shitting me, Sav?" Shaking his head, he's pissed, but I can tell, he's also worried about me. "What in the hell does he want?"

"I didn't know at first but when I was packing up to leave, I discovered what he was looking for. I've safely hidden it away again, as per Mum and Dad's request."

"What was it?"

"For your safety, Mike, I can't tell you. It's not that I don't trust you, but I can't risk Uncle Kelvin hurting you. He's had me attacked twice, who knows what he is capable of?"

"Let me help you then, I can call Officer Hamilton and she'll be able to do something."

"No!" I shout. "I don't want to involve anyone, especially not the police."

"You told me."

"Not by choice, had you not found me tonight, I never would have told you. Please just forget what you heard and forget you ever met me."

"Ha, that's not going to happen. I care about you, Sav. I want to help. Not sure what I can do, since you won't let me contact anyone, but I will do whatever is needed to keep you safe. The first thing I am going to do is get us another beer, have another shot, and then we will come up with a game plan."

Before I have a chance to say anything, he's in the kitchen getting our beers. I'm floored, I can't believe he wants to help me, be my hero, even though for the last few weeks, since Uncle Kelvin turned up, I've been such a bitch to him. Yet here he is, wanting to help, and he doesn't even know what I'm protecting or why. I watch him as he walks back into the lounge room and I smile. *Maybe I do need Mike Mustange on my team.*

He hands me the beer and pours us another round of shots. He looks at me and I can feel his stare all the way down in my soul. "Sav, I know there's more to the story, and I don't expect you to tell me everything now, but I hope that one day you will. In the meantime, I will do everything in my power to protect you. I can't explain it, but I'm drawn to you. I have this deep-seated need to help and protect you. Please, let me help you. Let me be your hero, Sav."

"Mike, no, I can't ask you to do that. My uncle is deranged and psychotic. He won't stop until I give him what he wants. Tonight he was scary; I have never seen him like that before. I can't risk him hurting you. I couldn't live with myself." Looking up, sadly I add, "Mike, as much as I want an 'us' there can't be an one, I won't risk you."

"Why don't you just give whatever he is looking for to him?"

"No! I can't!" I shout, "Mum and Dad specifically asked me not to in a letter they left for me. I will do everything in my power to honour their last wish."

"You are so stubborn but I understand why you are

doing this. We will just have to come up with another game plan then."

Mike and I sit on my couch, drinking beer and tequila, and it feels good to just forget everything for a few hours. After three-quarters of a bottle of tequila, and a few too many beers, I'm feeling pretty tipsy. I look over at Mike and the throb between my thighs starts up again. *Fuck he's gorgeous.*

Without even thinking, I lean over and kiss him. His lips are silky soft, yet rough at the same time, he tastes like tequila mixed with beer, uniquely Mike. I love it and I moan. Gently, I run my hands up his chest, I can feel his heart beating; it's beating in time with the throb in my pussy.

Pulling back, I realise that he wasn't kissing me back. I look towards my lap, feeling like a chump when I mumble, "Fuck it." I straddle his lap, place my hands on each of his cheeks, holding tight, and crash my lips against his. My tongue seeking entrance into his mouth and this time he opens up, our tongues mesh together in a slow exotic dance.

After one of the most intense kisses of my life, I pull back and stare deep into his eyes. "Mike, I want this, I want us. You're right. I can't let Uncle Kelvin dictate my life. I **KISS** want **KISS** you **KISS,** Mike."

"What about what you said before? And Uncle Asshat?"

"Ha, Uncle Asshat, I like that. Don't get me wrong, I'm scared shitless, Mike, but tonight, here with you, this here, it feels right." Smiling up at him, I continue, "You make me feel special and safe. When I'm with you the world around us ceases to exist and I absolutely love that. Will you have me, Mike Mustange?"

"Fuck yes, Savannah Blac, I'll have you any way I can." My face breaks out into the biggest smile. I'm staring at the gorgeous man in front of me and I could not be happier.

He looks deep into my soul, reaching up he gently caresses my cheek. "Right now though, I want you to wrap your arms around me and I want you to kiss me. Then I'm going to go home and let you think about all of this. I will be back in the morning, and if you still feel the same way as you do now, then I, Mike Francine Mustange, am going to make all of your dreams come true. Now, kiss me, woman."

Leaning forward, I wrap my arms around his shoulders and kiss him, quickly pulling back. I laugh, "Francine? Your middle name is Francine? That's the funniest shit ever."

"Yeah, it does suck, but it's a family name passed down to the first born. If you tell anyone, especially Kenz, I will go Al Capone on your ass."

"Whaaaat? Kenz doesn't know, how is that possible?"

"I'm just awesome, now, promise me you won't tell her."

"I promise, Mike Francine Mustange, your middle name is safe with me."

"Good, now kiss me again, woman."

Our lips crash together again and I'm lost in everything that is Mike; the world around me fades away. Mike and I kiss for what feels like hours but it is only a few minutes. I've never felt like this before; I'm scared and excited, all rolled into one horny, sexually, frustrated ball.

Rolling my hips, I feel his cock coming to life beneath me. I smile and start shamelessly grinding myself against his growing erection, moaning when it brushes against me. Reaching down, I stroke it through his shorts, but he grabs my wrist, halting me.

"Not tonight, Sav, I want you to be sure about this before I make love to you. You deserve to be treated like a princess. On that note, I'm going to go home and leave to you think about all of this."

I'm sad at the thought of him leaving, but I can see why he's doing it. I've completely changed my mind in the space of three hours, but I know that I want, no need. I need Mike in my life, and if this is what I need to do to prove to him, then reluctantly I'll do it. Mike is definitely worth the wait, what's another twelve hours anyway?

Grudgingly, I hop off his lap but he pulls me back down and kisses me again. He breaks our kiss and whispers, "Sav, I'll be back tomorrow morning, and I hope that you still feel this way. I've never felt like this with anyone before. I want you, Sav, more than anything. I want you to make sure this is what you want, because I guarantee that once your mine; you will never be alone, scared, or afraid of anything again. I will always be there for you, Sav, always."

"I want you too, Mike. I know I'm a hormonal, psycho bitch at the moment, but I finally know what I want, and it's you." Wrapping my arms around his waist, I get up on my tippy toes and I place a quick kiss on his lips before turning and walking to the door and opening it. "Now, out. I want you back here sooner rather than later."

Laughing, he walks towards the door and wraps his arms around me tightly and whispers, "You, my dear, are not a hormonal, psycho bitch. You are one sexy bitch, and I can't wait to make you mine tomorrow."

He kisses me on the cheek before slapping my ass and walking out the door. He's halfway down the front stairs when he turns and says, "Sweet dreams, Sav, think of me fucking you tomorrow."

Standing in my doorway, I'm left open-mouthed, shocked, and completely turned on. It's a struggle to not chase after him and mount him right there in my front yard. I watch him drive off before heading back inside and clearing up the empties.

After cleaning my teeth, I change into my sleep shorts and singlet. Grabbing my iPad, I start reading book two in the Affections series by Elizabeth Wills, *Mended Affections*. So glad that Kenz recommended this one to me. It's so emotional, but it's beautifully written at the same time, Elizabeth has a way with words that completely sucks you in and absorbs you.

Just as I'm about to turn the light off, my phone beeps with an incoming text.

Mike – *Nite princess. Can't wait to see you tomorrow*
Me – *Night handsome. I can't wait to ride you tomorrow, guess Buzz will have to do for now*

I giggle to myself at my teasing reply.

Mike – *Like hell you will. I will BUZZ the hell out of you you tomorrow with my cock ;P*

I laugh even harder at his reply and the throbbing between my thighs intensifies. *I can't wait for tomorrow,* I think to myself as I place my phone on the side table.

There is the biggest smile on my face, as I turn off the side lamp. I realise that I'm in love with Mike Francine Mustange.

34

MIKE

This past week has been one of the best. It all started when I left Sav's place in the wee hours of the morning last Saturday night, or Sunday morning...I never know with that shit. It killed me to leave, but I wanted her to be one-hundred-percent sure this is what she wanted. I couldn't handle being rejected again.

Sunday morning, I was back at her place at 10:00 a.m. When she opened the front door, she took my breath away—her bed hair was sexy, her sleepy eyes popped open, and they smiled. Yes, her eyes smiled, when she saw me, and her sexy mouth lifted into the biggest smile. Actually, I think she smiled at the coffee, but whatever, Sav is the sexiest woman I've ever met.

She invited me in and we sat apart on the couch, staring at each other, drinking our coffee, but not saying anything. The air was electric, neither of us quite sure how to act after our conversation last night. I know in my heart what I want, but I have to be cautious, I don't want to spook her. *I really want to be with Sav*, I think to myself as I take a sip of coffee.

Looking up, I see Sav staring at me and her smile is gorgeous. Running my hand back and forth over my smooth head, I say, "So, how you doing?"

"Did you just 'Joey' me, Mike?"

"Huh?" I look at her confused.

"Joey, from *Friends* he used to say, 'How you doin'?' when trying to hit on someone."

Laughing I reply, "Ha, he so did. No, wasn't my intention, but if it works, then hell yes, I'm 'Joey'ing' you."

Laughing she stands up, straddles my lap, and kisses me. Pulling back, she looks into my eyes and says, "You can 'Joey' my anytime, Mike." Leaning forward she kisses me again, I close my eyes and lose myself in this kiss.

The world stands still.

Everything around us ceases to exist.

It's just Sav and me.

I could not be happier right at this moment.

She pulls away and I feel lost, but looking at Sav, I see she is smiling, really smiling. I in turn cannot help but smile. Since I have known her, I don't think I have ever seen her smile like this; there is a spark in her eyes that I haven't seen before.

My cock starts to twitch; I start to feel embarrassed, but then I feel Sav ever so lightly rubbing herself on my growing erection. She wraps her arms around my neck, pulling me in closer, and kisses me with such force that our teeth crash together. Our lips are fused in one of the most emotion-filled kisses of my life.

Grabbing the hem of her of her shirt, I lift it over her head, and throw it on the floor. Raking my eyes over her chest, a low growl escapes my lips at the gorgeous sight before me. Her tits are covered in black lace and they look amazing. She smirks at me as she reaches behind her back and unclips her bra, lowering the straps slowly down her arms, before flicking it across the room.

Her tits were gorgeous encased in lace, but in all their naked glory, fuck me, they are stunning. Leaning forward, I wrap my lips around her nipple and suck it into my mouth, while pinching and rolling the other between my thumb and forefinger.

Arching her head and body, she shoves her tits further into my mouth, moaning in pleasure as I massage her breasts. Gently she runs her fingers over my head, groaning louder as I suck harder. "Fuck me now, Mike."

"Yes, ma'am."

She grabs my cheeks and stares deep into my eyes, "Don't." **KISS** "Ever." **KISS** "Call." **KISS** "Me." **KISS** "Ma'am." **KISS** "Again." **KISS** I don't get a chance to reply because all coherent thoughts escape me right at this moment. I'm mesmerized. Sav is striping off, clothes are flying across the room. My eyes rake over her naked body.

She reaches out to remove my pants and boxer briefs; my cock hardens further when I feel her fingers brush against my heated skin. She pushes me onto my back, lowering herself between my legs, taking my hard throbbing cock deep into her mouth and sucking; her tongue dancing around the tip. "Fuck, your mouth feels so good on my cock."

Sav mumbles something but I don't understand, as her mouth is full of my cock. Reaching a hand down, she starts to fondle my balls, while simultaneously grazing her teeth up my steel shaft. My eyes are closed. I'm close to coming when all of a sudden; I feel her pinkie pushing against my asshole. Immediately, my eyes dart open and I look down to see Sav staring at me. I'm lost in her beauty until I feel her edging her finger in deeper. Before I can say anything, I'm coming down her throat, her finger pushing in deeper, as I have the most intense orgasm of my life.

Once she has sucked every last drop, she kisses her way up my chest. Nipping my nipples before straddling me and kissing me deeply.

"That was amazing, Sav. I have never come so hard in my life."

She giggles before kissing me again. Pulling back she whispers as she starts to grind my cock. "I'm going to fuck you now, Mike."

Even though I have just come, my dick immediately springs back to life. Sav lifts up, and gently lowers herself over my shaft, taking it all the way to the hilt. We fall into a rhythm that feels like nothing I have felt before.

Reaching up, I pull her to me and kiss her deeply as she continues to ride my cock. Sitting up, she starts to ride me faster, sliding up and down. Her hands go to her tits and she starts tugging on them, it's the hottest sight that I have ever seen. We play with her tits together before she guides my hand down to her clit; together we tug and pull at her swollen nub.

"I'm close, Mike," she breathlessly says.

Increasing her thrusts, together our orgasms take over our bodies and we shout out each other's names as I come for the second time this morning. Once our orgasm has subsided, she falls on top of me. I wrap my arms around her, hugging her close to my body.

When our breathing returns to normal, she climbs off me, and snuggles into my side. We don't say anything, it's not awkward; it's perfect. In this moment, I realise that I have strong feelings for Sav.

We are lying in each other's arms on her couch, still panting from another marathon sexcapade when there is a knock at the door. We both groan, we don't want to have to get up but the knocking continues. Reluctantly, I get up, pull on my shorts, and head to the door.

Opening the door, I see that no one on the porch, but there is a box sitting on the doormat with 'Savannah Blac' written on the top. Bending down, I pick it up, and bring it inside, placing it on the coffee table, just as Sav sits up and pulls her singlet over her head. I inwardly sigh as her gorgeous tits are now covered, but she's not wearing a bra, so I can still see her nipples. As I sit down next to her, I reach over and give one a pinch.

Smacking my arm, she squeals, "Ouch, what was that for?"

"Just saying 'hi' to the girls, they look lonely and sad to be covered by your top." I pause. "I know for a fact, the girls love hanging freely in the wind."

"You're a fiend, Mike Francine Mustange, but the girls thank you for the attention. If you play your cards right, they might come out for a visit again very soon." She winks at me, before looking towards the box.

Scooting towards the edge of the couch, she opens the package and gasps. Inside there are empty packets of Skittles, empty beer bottles and flowers, torn to shreds. Sav immediately bursts into tears and wraps her arms around me. I pull her closer to me, hugging her tight and rubbing circles on her back to calm her down. Her sobs have now overtaken her body and she's shaking in fear.

She eventually calms down, grabs the box, opens her front door, and heads downstairs, disposing of the package in the garbage bins. She slams the front door behind her and sits back down next to me. Taking a deep breath, she looks towards me. "That was a package from Uncle Kelvin."

"What the fuck?"

"Those three items were Mum, Dad, and Jace's fav. He sent a similar package a few weeks ago, but this time he's shredded the flowers and sent empties. I can't trust a word that he said last night, and this just confirms my decision to not give him what he wants."

"Are you sure that's wise? He seems pretty fucked up, if you ask me. Sav. I don't want anything to happen to you."

"I'm sure, Mike. I promise I'll handle this." Jumping up, she turns to me, smiles seductively, rips her shirt over her head, turns around, and heads towards the bedroom. When she passes the kitchen, she asks over her shoulder, "Are you coming?"

Jumping up, I stalk over to her, wrap my arms around her waist, pulling her tightly against my chest and whisper into her ear, "You and I will both be coming very shortly."

She turns her head back to me and I kiss her. My hand sliding and tickling its way up her tight tummy before massaging her tits, tugging and pulling on her pert pink nipples as I increase the kiss. She turns around and wraps her arms around my neck, pulling us closer together. Our lips fuse in one of the most passionate kisses of my life.

My hands find their way under her ass and I lift her up. She wraps her legs around my waist and I make my way to her bedroom. As I lower her to the bed, I growl, "We are not leaving this bed for the next twelve hours. I'm going to make love to you and worship every inch of your body."

She shimmies out of her undies before seductively saying, "Well, what are you waiting for?" She pulls on her own nipples, closing her eyes, and moaning. Seeing her play with her tits is the hottest thing I've ever seen, and each time is hotter than the last.

Quickly I strip off my pants before jumping onto the bed next to her. Leaning down, I take one of her nipples in my mouth and suck, grazing my teeth along the tip before sucking it again. Sav's back arches, she grips the sheets tightly and moans, shoving her beautiful tits further into my face. I lose myself in her tits, her moans getting louder and louder, increasing the hardness growing between my legs.

Looking down at Sav, I line my throbbing cock up at her entrance and slowly enter the tip before pulling back out again. She whimpers each time I do this; she starts to lift off the bed and then I plunge my cock deep inside her. We both moan, her pussy clenching my cock as I thrust in and out.

"Ohh, Mike," Sav moans, "I'm close."

Picking up speed, I pump harder and faster into her. Before I know it, we are both tumbling over the edge, as our orgasms erupt. I'm grunting my release and Sav is quaking under me. I collapse on top of her, both of us panting, gasping for air.

Once our breathing has evened out, I roll off of her and she snuggles into my side. I wrap my arms around her, pulling her closer to me. I start running my hands up and down her arm. I have never felt this content and happy.

We spend the rest of Sunday naked, lazing around together, eating Kung Fu Palace, and fucking like rabbits. It was the perfect day and the best way to end the weekend.

Sav and I have decided to keep our new relationship on the down low, for the meantime, well until we can come up with a game plan for Uncle Kelvin. It will be hard to keep my hands off her when we are around others, but she thinks it's safer this way, and I want her to be happy...I'd probably agree with anything to make her happy.

Personally, I think we need to call the police but Sav is adamant that this is not to happen. She wants to deal with this herself; man she is stubborn. Maybe I can covertly speak to Office Hamilton and get some pointers. It really bugs me that this asshole is doing this to Sav, but I will do everything in my power to protect her.

35

KELVIN

THAT LOOK, I KEEP PLAYING IT OVER AND OVER IN MY head: priceless. It was pure shock when she saw me, I could not be happier. Well, I could be, if the little bitch would just give me what's mine. I've given her a week.

This morning, I dropped off another package, just before lunch. This time I stuck around to see her reaction, but that bald dude picked it up and took it inside. However a few minutes later, the door flung open, and she raced down to the bin and dumped it. Watching her, my smile falters, I realised that there was no fear on her face whatsoever. "Fuck!" I shout into the car. *I need to up my game. I refuse to lose what's rightfully mine.*

I'm really pissed off that she's not caving. So I decide that everyday until I approach her again, I'm going to send her packages. Deciding to send them to both her home and work, I'm going to rattle her until she caves.

As I'm driving away after arranging this week's deliveries, the best of the best ideas pops into my head. The little whore seems to be getting chummy with that baldheaded twat. Whenever he leaves her place, he always has a super big smile on his face. If she doesn't cave after my ultimatum, I know how I can get what's mine.

I'm an evil genius, I think to myself, phase two is perfect.

36

SAV

THIS WEEK HAS BEEN BOTH UNBELIEVABLY AWESOME and at the same time, unbelievably shitty. Uncle Kelvin seems to have upped his mind games by sending me daily packages; to both home and work. I'm trying not to let him get to me, but it's hard. Luckily I have Mike on my team.

Mike has been over every night but he hasn't stayed over. When I'm around him, I'm happy. I haven't felt happiness like this since before Mum, Dad, and Jace died. I'm sad that they won't get to know and meet Mike, but I know they would be happy for me.

I'm not going to be seeing Mike tonight as he's watching the twins for Kenz and Jordan. Not going to lie, I'm sad but I'm also looking forward to a long soak in the tub, a block of *Cadbury's Snack Chocolate* and *Orange is The New Black* on Netflix.

Just as I'm heading to the bathroom to run the bath, my phone pings with a text.

Kenz – *Hey lovely. Are you free tonight to check in on Mike as he's watching the girls...solo*
Me – *No concrete plans. Happy to check in on him*
Kenz – *Thanks. Don't tell him I sent you*
Me – *Your secret is safe with me*

I do a happy dance as I head to my bedroom. An evil and sexy idea pops into my head as I strip off and get changed.

Forty minutes later, I pull up at Kenzie and Jordan's place, just as they are walking over to Jordan's Jeep. "Hey guys," I say as I walk towards them. They both turn around; Jordan's mouth drops open and Kenzie's eye pop wide.

Jordan wolf whistles and I smile. "Woo Woo, Sav. You look smokin' hot. Do you have a hot date tonight?"

My cheeks heat a shade of pink. "Maybe," I squeak out, thinking to myself that maybe this outfit was a bad idea. I'm wearing skinny jeans and a black deep V halter-top, which really makes my girls look amazing, and black wedge sandals.

Kenzie looks at me knowingly and walks over, wraps her arms around me, and whispers, "You and I soooo need to talk, I need the Sav and Mike goss." Pulling back, I'm shaking my head as if to say 'nothing is going on' but Kenzie gives me her 'Kenzie stare,' and I can't help but smile. I mouth, "Next week" and wink.

She turns towards the car, "Come on, Jor, let's go." She turns back to me. "We were just heading out but

Mike's here watching the girls. If you want to say hi. I know you want Rory cuddles and I know they'd love to see Aunty Sav." I don't miss her smug remark.

"Are you sure it's okay? I actually came to see you too, Kenz."

"Yeah, I'm sure. We can catch up for coffee next week." Winking at me, she adds, "Just behave." *Bitch*, I think to myself as turn and head towards the front door. Taking a deep breath, I slowly make my way to the house.

My heart is erratically beating.

I'm nervous.

I'm excited.

I feel like a schoolgirl as I raise my hand and knock on the door.

37

MIKE

I'VE JUST CRACKED A BEER AND PULLED UP *BOLD AND the Beautiful* on the *Telstra* box when there's a knock at the door. Sighing, I pause and go to the door. Opening it, I'm left stunned when I see Sav standing there...she looks fucking hot. "Hey, gorgeous, what are you doing here?"

"Well, I heard you were babysitting, and I thought that you might like some company."

"I'll take any time I can get with you." Reaching out, I wrap my arms around her waist and kiss her. Our lips crashing, tongues entwining together, she moans into my mouth, and it goes straight to my cock. Pulling back, I look deep into her eyes. "We need to stop that, otherwise I won't be held accountable for what I do next, and I don't think the neighbours will appreciate what I have in mind."

Giggling, she steps past me and starts pissing herself laughing. Looking towards the TV, I see her staring at what's paused on the screen. *Ohh shit*, I think to myself, *how am I going to explain Bold being paused on the TV?*

"What's so funny?" I decide to play dumb.

"Ummm, you watch *Bold*?"

"Yep." I let the p in yep pop.

"Are you serious?"

"Yep, I'm not ashamed to admit it, well maybe to Jordan, but yes I watch *Bold* and I love it."

"Hmmpf, I would have pegged you as more of a *Days of Our Lives* fan."

"My Nana and I used to watch this when I was in high school and she'd come to visit. I got hooked, and after she passed away, I started watching it again, it's now my secret guilty pleasure."

"That's sweet but I'm totally telling Jordan, this is too good to keep a secret."

"Like fuck you are!" I yell and I must do it a smidge too loud as one of the girls cries. "Fuck. Wait here and I'll go and settle her."

Thankfully, Indi goes straight back to sleep after a quick back rub. When I come back out, Sav is sitting on the couch, sipping on her own beer and she pats the couch next to her. "Come here, spunky, and we can watch *Bold* together. I promise not to share your dirty little secret but it's going to cost you."

Sitting down next to her, I grab my beer and she snuggles into me. "So, what's it going to cost me to keep this secret?"

She glances over at me, "I haven't decided yet but I'll be sure to let you know when I do. Now shh, I bet Brooke is about to say something very really, super duper important."

"Don't sass Brooke, Sav. Or I will have to punish you."

Sav seductively looks at me as she leans forward to grab her beer, giving me a perfect view down her top. "Maybe I want to be punished, Mike."

"Ohh, when we leave here, you will be punished... with my cock... repeatedly...all night long."

"Bring it!" she huskily says, winking at me before turning her attention back at the TV.

———

Sav and I have a nice, relaxing night together, hanging out and watching the girls; seriously these two munchkins are the cutest babies in the whole entire world. We eat pizza, drink beer, and chat, getting to know each other better. Everything is comfortable with Sav and we don't once mention her uncle.

We end up making out on Kenzie and Jordan's couch, and we are so wrapped up in each other that we don't hear them come home. We don't notice anything until we hear Jordan squeal like a girl, "Ouch, fuck, Kenz, what was that for?" He rubs his arm right where Kenz punched him.

"Told you they'd be doing it when we got home."

We both immediately sit up, feeling like we've been caught by our parents. We look at each other and burst out laughing. I shift Sav off my lap; while Kenz and Jordan snuggle on the chaise together. Kenz looks at us, wiggling her eyebrows. "So, how was your evening?"

In unison we say, "Great!"

"Okay, you two, cut the crap, when did you...this happen?" She's spinning her finger in circles, pointing at us.

Getting up, I head to the kitchen and come back with four beers. After handing them out, I sit next to Sav and she snuggles into my side. I lean towards her and place a gentle kiss on the side of her head. Sav quietly sighs as I do this, garnering a "Naw!" from Kenz.

Sav snuggles in closer; I tighten my hold on her. She rests her hand on my thigh, and her finger runs back and forth, her touch causing my cock to stir; I can't help but smile.

Looking up, I see Kenz and Jordan are staring intently towards us. Jordan gives me a subliminal high five and subtly toasts his beer towards me. Kenz is bubbling with excitement; she can hardly sit still. "I'm waiting, guys. Spill. Now."

Sav and I both laugh at her enthusiasm and we give the *Cliff Notes* version of the last week, leaving out all the Uncle Kelvin crap. Gauging from the super big smile on both of their faces, I'd say that they are happy for us.

We have a few more beers with them before we call it a night. Sav decides to stay at my place, but first we swing by her duplex to drop off her car and get a change of clothes...not that she'll be wearing anything.

We get to her place and she quickly races inside. Feeling like a perv, I lean against my car, watching her as she skips up the stairs, and wolf whistle at her sexy ass, those pants mold to her perfectly. I can't wait to strip her out of them. She emphasises swinging her ass from side to side as she gets near the top of the stairs, and my cock starts to stir. She turns and blows me a kiss before she ducks inside. I have to adjust myself, as it's getting uncomfortable in my jeans.

I decide it's safer for me to wait down here if we are to make it back to my place. It's better that I don't go inside, otherwise we'd never make it to Casa del Mike.

I'm staring up at the sky and I realise that I'm genuinely happy, a feeling that I haven't known in a very longtime. I haven't felt like this since for she-devil and I know it's all to do with the hottie upstairs. I'm so lost in that thought, I don't notice a person coming up behind me.

Just as I register their presence, they whack me across the back of the head, and I stumble forward. Before I have a chance to react, they hit me again, and I fall to the ground. The last thing I see, before I black out, is a menacing figure standing over me, laughing to himself.

SAV

When I come to, my vision is fuzzy and my head is throbbing, so I close my eyes again. I feel like I drank an entire bottle of tequila and have the hangover from hell. "Ugh!" I moan. All of a sudden, my eyes flip open and I realise; I'm tied to a chair in a room, with newspaper covering the windows. The paint is cracking and peeling and it smells musty. My eyes wander around the room and they fall upon Mike, on the floor in the corner, his arms are tied behind his back and his legs are bound; I start to panic.

"Mike!" I shout but he doesn't move. I try to get to him but I can't. "Mike!" I shout again. This time he stirs and I begin to cry. "Mike," I blubber. "Mike, can you hear me?"

"Sav?" he groans and slowly opens his eyes. When he sees me strapped to the chair, his eyes pop open wide, and he tries to sit up but winces in pain. "Fuck, my ribs."

Mike rolls onto his side and winces again; he manages to get up into a sitting position and looks around. His eyes landing on me again. I burst into tears when I see the dried blood on the side of his face.

"Mike, you're bleeding. Are you okay?"

He stammers, "I...I...I don't know. My heads hurts like a bitch and my ribs, I think one's broken." Pausing, he looks over at me. "Don't worry about me. Are you okay, Sav?"

"I think so. What happened? Where are we?"

"The last thing I remember is watching your ass as you went into your duplex and thinking that I can't wait to get you back to my place. Then there's nothing until I heard you call out for me, just now. How about you?"

"It's all fuzzy, Mike. The last thing I remember to leaving Kenzie and Jordan's, everything after that is blank." The tears stream down my face and I start to hyperventilate.

The door to the room opens with a thud and I jump in fright. Looking up, I freeze when I see who is standing there. I whisper, "Uncle Kelvin?"

"Morning, sunshine," he says, as he slams the door behind him, again I jump in fear.

"What's going on? Where are we?"

He doesn't answer me, he just manically laughs. He walks over to Mike and stands on his wrist; Mike screams out in pain. I yell and plead for him to stop, but he just continues to laugh and press his foot down harder.

"Tell me what I want and I will leave loverboy alone."

"I...I..."

"Don't tell him, Sav," Mike says through gritted teeth. Uncle Kelvin lifts his foot off Mike's hand, turns around, swings his leg back and kicks Mike in the ribs, repeatedly. Mike grunts in pain, wincing each time the boot collides with his side. I'm begging for Uncle Kelvin to stop but he keeps kicking Mike, over and over.

"Shut your God damn mouth, boy. This is a family matter."

"Fuck you, you psychotic piece of shit. When I get out of here, you are going down. Now let Sav go."

Uncle Kelvin ignores Mike and walks over to me. He leans on the arms of the chair, gets right in my face, his breath causing me to gag, and sneers, "Tell me where it is and I'll leave you both alone, it's up to you. I've got all the time in the world."

The tears start to roll down my face again. I look over to Mike; he looks like he's struggling to breathe. Uncle Kelvin grabs my chin roughly. "This can all be over in an instant, just tell me where the fuck it is."

I'm torn right at this moment, I want to honour Mum and Dad's wishes, but at the same time, I want him to stop punishing Mike. I can't speak; the sobs have over-taken my body. It only pisses him off further. He stands up and slaps me hard across the cheek, knocking me and the chair over. I land on the ground with a thud and see stars when my head hits the floor.

"Fucking stubborn bitch," he snarls, as he turns and walks out of the room. Slamming the door behind him.

When I come to, Mike has my managed to get himself free and untie me from the chair. My head is resting on his thigh, and he is gently running his fingers through my hair.

Smiling, I stare up at him, and for a moment, I forget

about the hell that we are in. Then it all comes crashing back to me. I take in a deep breath and begin to cry again.

"Shhhh, don't cry, Sav, we'll be okay. I'll get us out of here."

"How, Mike? This is my entire fault. I knew I should have stayed away from you. I'm sooo sorry, Mike, so, so sorry."

"Shhhh, it's going to be fine."

"I hope so, Mike, how are we free?"

"Uncle Douche isn't very good with knots. I managed to wriggle and twist free." Lifting up his wrist I see that it's red, inflamed, and bleeding slightly.

"Ohh, Mike, your wrist." Lifting his wrist, I place a gentle kiss just below the redness.

He smiles down at me and whispers, "All better now." His smile is calming; I lay back down in his lap, staring up at him.

We sit there quietly for a few moments. I shuffle into a sitting position when I feel something in my back pocket. I realise that I have my phone. I'm thankful that my uncle didn't find it when he took us. Just as I go to tell Mike, the door crashes open with a bang.

"Ohh look, the two lovebirds are up." He marches into the room and grabs me by my hair, wrenching me off Mike, before throwing me into the corner. I brace for the impact but it still takes the wind out of me. He storms over to me and lifts me into a sitting position, squeezing my upper arms tightly, getting in my face he demands, "Have you comes to your senses yet?"

Mike yells, "Sav, don't tell him! You're strong, think of your parents."

He turns towards Mike. "Shut the fuck up, punk."

"Punk?" Mike taunts him, "No one says punk anymore, douche. Now leave her the fuck alone."

He stalks over to Mike, bends down, and pulls out his penknife. Flicking the blade out; he stabs it into his thigh, twisting it around. Mike screams in pain, I scream for Mike and Uncle Kelvin laughs, a manic sound that grates through me.

Looking at Mike in pain, I start to uncontrollably sob. I knew this would happen and now the person that I'm in love with is suffering because of me.

Uncle Kelvin slashes Mike's legs and arms over and over, yelling. "Just fucking tell me!" I can see Mike is in horrendous pain and my heart is breaking, but I can't speak. I'm heaving to breathe and I feel like I'm about to pass out again, but I need to stay awake. Mike is being so tough, gritting his teeth, trying to not let my uncle see how much it hurts. He finally stops torturing Mike and as he stands up, he licks the blade clean while he stares directly at me.

I'm cowering in the corner, fearful that he will start slashing me next; the tears continue to flow down my cheeks. He points the knife at me. "I'll give you one more chance, you little bitch, tell me what I want or next time the cuts won't be so gentle." Pausing, he walks over, squats down in front of me, grips my chin roughly, and says in a calm. menacing voice. "And then you will be responsible for his demise." He pokes me in the chest as he says this, before getting up and slamming the door on his way out.

Immediately, I crawl over to Mike. Ripping my shirt

off, I wipe at all the cuts and then I wrap it around his leg where he dug the knife in to try and stop the blood flow. I get the improvised tourniquet tied and wrap my arms around Mike. "I'm so sorry, baby. I will fix this, I promise."

He wraps his arms around me and pulls me closer, flinching as he does. "For a short fucker, he sure is strong," Mike says. I sit cross-legged next to him when I remember the phone in my pocket. I look over my shoulder to make sure the door is closed and I slip it out.

Mike's eyes widen and he encourages me with his eyes. He whispers, "Text Kenz to contact Kelly."

Sav – *Help us Kenz. Text Kelly. We are in trouble*

Immediately my phone rings but thankfully it was on silent. I quickly answer and don't give her a chance to talk, "Kenz, I can't explain but Mike and I need help. He says Kelly will be able to track and find us, please hurry."

For the first time ever, Kenz doesn't argue or ask questions. She says okay and be safe before hanging up.

Just as I have put my phone back in my pocket, the door swings open again but he doesn't come in. He throws two bottles of water towards us and then slams the door shut again.

Mike and I sit there staring at the bottles of water. I'm beyond parched but I'm not game to eat or drink anything that he gives us. Who knows what it will be laced with?

The day continues along same path; he comes

barreling in, threatens me, tortures Mike. I've almost caved so many times, but each time I go to speak, Mike steps in and stops me.

Mike looks like he is about to pass out, and I decide that the next time I'll tell him. Mum and Dad will understand; I can't let this go on. No sooner have I finished that thought, the door once again slams open, and I think, *it's now or never*.

39

KELVIN

THIS COULD NOT BE GOING ANY BETTER. I GET TO torture loverboy, and I can see that I'm slowly breaking down her walls. She will be telling me exactly what I want to know, in no time at all.

This torturing gig is actually fun, tiring but fun. I was shocked at how easy it was to stab into his flesh. I thought the knife would struggle but it slid in so easy. Surprisingly, it was harder nicking his arms and legs. Her screams spurred me on, though. I'm impressed at how tough this bastard is, he never passed out once.

Deciding to play with them, I open the door and stand there. The late afternoon sunlight shining behind me, leaves me as an ominous figure in silhouette. After staring at them, I toss a couple bottles of water into the room. I don't say a word; the only sound is the bottles hitting the concrete floor. Neither of them moves, they just cower and huddle in the corner together, pussies.

She looks frightened and he doesn't look too well at all; his face is pasty and he looks like he has a fever. That makes me smile and I know it won't be long until I get what I want. Tuning my back on them, I slam the door and snicker as I walk away.

I'm sitting in the adjoining room, watching a movie, and I start to cackle to myself. If only dear old sissy could see me now, she would be rolling over in her grave; this makes my laughs increase. If she had just given me what I wanted in the beginning, none of this would have had to happen; she'd still be alive and I could be sitting on a beach in Thailand. *Soon that can happen*, I think to myself, as I laugh and laugh.

Jumping up, I decide that I've had enough of this shit, I don't want to wait any longer. I'm going to end this once and for all. I'm determined to get the location and finally I will get what is mine... nothing will stop me now.

40

MIKE

Sav and I have been here for what feels like days, yet it's only been half a day. I'm hoping and praying Kenzie gets the message to Kelly; I'm not sure how much more I can withstand. All I know is that I have to be strong for Sav. We are huddling in the corner, staring at the water bottles. I really want to drink that water but I'm pretty sure he has laced it with something, and I need to stay awake and alert if I'm to protect her.

She is starting to shake from fear; I wrap my arm tighter around her, even though the cuts hurt like a bitch every time I move. I'm rubbing her arm gently, hoping to sooth her. "Hey, Sav, did you know that when I was little, I used to think that at night time, sharks would swim through the pool filter and into our pool?"

She pulls away from me, totally confused. "What?"

"When I was little, I used to think that sharks..."

"Yeah, I heard that but why in the hell are you telling me that?"

"I wanted to take your mind off this, and that's the first thing that came to mind."

Laughing, she says, "Well, when I was little I used to call my elbow an oboe."

"Well, I used to call the fire trucks, firefucks and I'd shout out at the top of my lungs 'Look, Mum, a firefuck' whenever I saw one. She was so embarrassed and would cover my mouth if we saw one."

"I bet you were a total shit of a kid." I just stare at her and smile. "I take from your nonanswer that I am correct." She pauses and adds, "I was a complete..." But she doesn't get a chance to answer because Kelvin kicks open the door and barges into the room.

Looking up at him, I see he has a gun in his hand and it's pointed directly at Sav. My heart literally stops beating, and I reach out to grab Sav's hand; she is now shaking uncontrollably.

"You ready to talk, bitch?"

I push Sav behind me to try and protect her.

"Ohh, how sweet, loverboy is trying to protect you. It won't do any good, though. As soon as I get the location and get what's mine, there's a bullet for each of you in here. Now, last chance, bitch, where the fuck are they?"

Sav is still behind me and she has completely zoned out, she looks catatonic, just staring into space, tears pouring down her face. My heart is breaking for her.

Kelvin shoves me out of the way and slaps Sav across the face, but she still just stares into space. I land with a thud and the pain in my thigh from the gouge is unbearable. Blood immediately starts pouring down my leg as the wound opens up. I manage to pull myself up onto my knees, just as Kelvin points to gun towards Sav's head. I yell, "Noooooooo!" and I charge for him, knocking him over, the two of us crashing to the floor.

The gun slides across the cement and lands just near the door. I scramble over to get it, but Kelvin jumps on my back and slams my head into the concrete a few times. I start to see stars and feel like I'm about to pass out.

He climbs off me and grabs the gun, pointing it at Sav once again. "Last time, bitch, where's my gems?"

Sav is still staring into space and this only pisses him off further. He takes a step closer when we hear a noise in the other room, and someone yelling "Police!" He looks towards the door, confused. While he is preoccupied, I take the chance and jump up; Kelvin turns and fires the gun.

BANG!

The last thing I hear as we both crash to the ground is Sav screaming my name, and then darkness takes over me.

IT'S BEEN THREE DAYS SINCE WE WERE RESCUED.

It's been three days since Uncle Kelvin was arrested.

It's been three days and Mike has yet to wake up.

When Mike charged my uncle, he pulled the trigger, and Mike was shot in the shoulder. The bullet went straight through but he lost a lot of blood, and he lost consciousness. They managed to stop the bleeding, but he won't wake up.

I've been by his bedside for the past three days, and I won't be leaving until he wakes up, and I know he's okay. Kenz and Jordan have been by daily, but it's hard for them to stay with the girls. They keep trying to get me to go home, but I'm not leaving Mike. He's here because of me. I told myself that this would happen and now he is unconscious, lying in a hospital bed...because of me.

I knew Uncle Kelvin was a psychotic dickwad but I didn't realise how psycho he really was. Turns out, he was behind the 'accident' that killed Mum, Dad, and

Jace. He also admitted that he hired the thugs back home and here to scare me. He was pissed off that everything was left to me when they died. Little does he know, that even if I had died too, Mum and Dad never left him the gems anyway. All belongings were to be auctioned off and the funds donated to the Heart Foundation. Either way, he was screwed.

I get satisfaction knowing that he will be rotting in jail until his trial, and for the rest of his miserable life. He has officially been charged with the murder of Mum, Dad, and Jace, two counts of kidnapping, kidnapping causing grievous bodily harm, and for orchestrating the attacks on me.

That gives me comfort, but I will be much happier when Mike wakes up. What I wouldn't give to see his beautiful blue eyes staring back at me, followed by him saying something really inappropriate.

"Please wake up, Mike," I whisper.

Resting my head on the edge of his bed, I grab his hand and squeeze it, like I have for the past three days, and I start to cry, again. Deep down I knew this was going to happen, and now that it has, I feel terrible.

"This is all my fault, it should be me in this bed." The tears overtake my body. "Please wake up, Mike." **SOB**. "I'm so, so sorry." **SOB.** "I love you, Mike." **SOB.** "Please don't leave me." **SOB.**

"I love you too, Sav."

My head shoots up and I see his bright baby blue eyes staring at me, and I start to cry again. "Mike, you're awake. Thank God!" Jumping up, I wrap my arms around him, and I feel him wince in pain. I quickly pull away and sit back down. Grabbing his hand, I squeeze it tight, he squeezes it back and I start to cry again. "I'm so sorry this happened to you, Mike. This is all my fault."

"Shhhh, babe, don't cry. It's not your fault, but can you fill me in on what happened? The last thing I remember is dickwad pointing a gun towards you."

Before I get a chance to tell him what happened, the nurse comes into the room. She asks me to leave so she can assess Mike. I head out into the corridor just as Kenz, Jordan, and the girls arrive. I run up to Kenz. "He's awake!" I smile and shout.

"Ohh, thank God for that," Kenz says in relief as she hugs me, and Indi pokes her finger up my nose. I laugh, "Hello to you, too, gorgeous." I turn and give Jordan and Rory a hug, too. "The nurse is in with him at the moment."

We all take a seat in the corridor while we wait. It's awkward, I feel like they are judging and blaming me; I don't blame them really. It is entirely my fault.

Now that Mike is awake, I'm really nervous to be around him and his friends. I know he said he loves me too, but he's high on drugs right now. I know he hates me. This all happened because of me. The awkwardness is killing me, so I quickly jump up and tell Kenz and Jordan that I have to go. Before they can protest, I turn and run down the corridor.

By time I get to my car, the tears are pouring down my face and I'm a sobbing mess. Sliding down the side of my car, I cry uncontrollably, wrapping my arms around my knees, hugging myself. The tears finally subside and I contemplate going back inside, but I can't face them, not yet. I need time to wrap my head around everything, but most of all, I need to figure out how to say goodbye to the only man I have ever loved.

42

MIKE

When I wake up, Sav is resting her head on my bed crying. I hear her say she loves me; it makes me all warm and fuzzy to hear that so I whisper back, "I love you too, Sav." Her head shoots up and her face is broken, but she has a big smile on her face. She throws her arms around me and it hurts like a motherfucker, that's when I realise I'm in a hospital bed. My shoulder hurts just as badly as my leg does, but before I can get any answers the nurse walks in.

Before I know it, Sav is gone and I'm being poked and prodded. The nurse tells me that I was shot and have been unconscious for the past three days. *Three days, fuck me.* Thankfully everything seems to be healing fine and there shouldn't be any permanent damage. Just before she leaves she says that the doctor will be along soon.

As she is leaving, I ask her to send Sav back in. She quietly closes the door and I close my eyes again. When I hear the door open and I look towards the door smiling, my smile falters when I see Jordan and Kenz walk in, sans Sav.

"It's nice to see you awake, Sleeping Beauty," Jordan says, and he comes over to the bed and takes a seat.

Kenz walks around to the other side. "I'm so glad you're okay, Mike, you gave us all quite a scare."

I'm not really listening as I'm still staring at the door, waiting for Sav to come back in. "Where's Sav?"

Kenz and Jordan look between themselves warily when Kenz tells me, "Umm, she left."

"The fuck?" I realise they have the twins with them. "Sorry, munchkins, what the fire truck? Did she say if she's coming back?"

"Sorry, Mike, she didn't say anything."

I'm gutted that she left without saying goodbye, and if I know Sav, which I'm pretty sure that I do, she will be blaming herself over this. Now she's going to shut me out. *Well, I don't think so, love, I've worked too hard to get you to open up and let me in.* I know without a doubt; we are meant to be together. I will do everything in my power to prove that to Sav, I feel it in my bones. Now that Uncle Asshat is out of the picture, there's nothing stopping us. Speaking of Kelvin. "What happened to Uncle Douche?"

"Well, he shot you and he's currently rotting in jail." Pausing, Kenz adds, "It also turns out that he was responsible for the car accident that killed Sav's family, so he's being charged with that, too. Kelly and Officer Ferguson will be by later to talk to you and get your statement."

"Crikey dick. No wonder Sav is freaking out. How is she?"

"She's pretty upset up and confused right now, Mike."

Jordan adds, "I can't imagine how she's feeling right now. Knowing your uncle killed your family then he almost killed you, too. And all over a handful of rare gems."

"So, that's what he was after. Sav would never tell me, she said it was safer that way." A light bulb goes off in my head. "Is she Savannah Blac from the Blac Family Jewelers chain?"

They both nod. "Yep, that's the one dude," Jordan says.

Kenz adds, "Your girlfriend is the sole owner of the second biggest jewelry chain in Australia. Her family is jewelry royalty in this country." She looks to Jordan and then continues, "The gems that her uncle wanted are really rare and have been passed down for generations. He wanted them to sell and clear a massive gambling debt. Hence, trying to bump everyone off."

"Fuck! What a bastard. Kenz, I'm going to need your help."

"Sure, anything, Mike, you know that. What do you need?"

"I need you to help me win Sav back. I know her and she's going to pull away because she feels guilty for what happened to me. I'll bet my left nut, she feels fuckin' guilty that she survived and her family didn't. She's going to push everyone away and take off, again. I can't let her leave." I try to sit up, so I can get out of bed to go and see her, but the pain in my shoulder is unbearable. "Fuck!" I wince in pain.

"Kenz, please go to Sav. Make sure she doesn't do anything stupid and rash. See if you can get her to come and see me. I need to see her." Quietly, I add, "I love her."

Both Kenz and Jordan's mouths pop open in shock and in unison they say, "Fuck me dead said Foreskin Fred."

Kenz is still frozen in shock, when Jordan says, "I knew you liked her, but love her, wow, Mike. I thought after the she-devil you would never love another."

"I know, right? But there is something about Sav, I think I knew it from the first time she served me at the Dungeon. The first time I saw her, I knew she was it for me. She's special and I will do anything to keep her here."

...I remember the first day I saw her. It was a Tuesday night, and as usual, I was sitting at the bar throwing back tequila with a beer chaser when she walked in. The rest of the room faded away and the lights behind the bar bathed her in a beautiful glow. My God she was stunning. She looked over towards me and smiled; my heart melted. Then our eyes locked for the first time and it was magical. I could feel her stare deep within in my soul and it warmed me. She smiled at me again and I couldn't help but smile back. I'm pretty sure we both felt a magnetic pull in that moment.

I was done for, and even though I had sworn off women, I knew in that moment that I needed to get to know this angel. After that night, I found any excuse to go to the Dungeon, and if I didn't see her, I felt empty. Even if I just saw her in passing and we didn't chat, it was enough to keep me going until the next time.

I think I was in love with her from our first meeting.

. . .

"Naw, Mike's, in loooove." Hearing Kenz say that pulls me back into reality. I look over at her and she is smiling at me like the cat that caught the canary. "Told you, you'd find the one. Now, let's come up with a game plan to keep our girl here."

I knew I could count on Kenz. It's time to win over my girl!

"Please, Kenz," I plead. "I can't lose her."

43

SAV

It's been five days since shit went down with Uncle Kelvin, and it's been two days since I've seen Mike. I feel so guilty for all that happened to him so I have stayed away. I just wish that I had followed my gut instinct and kept to myself. If I had, then Mike would not be lying in a hospital bed, recovering from being tortured and shot.

Rolling over in bed, I sigh. I guess, the only positive about this is that Uncle Kelvin is behind bars...where he belongs. I was devastated to learn that he was behind the car accident that killed my family, all because he wanted the family gems. I can't believe this all happened over a handful of jewels.

Climbing out of bed, I head towards the kitchen for a much-needed cup of coffee. Entering my kitchen I sigh, coffee reminds me of Mike, and thinking of Mike reminds me that due to my family, he's currently in a hospital bed. At that thought, a lone tear falls down my cheek and I whisper, "I'm so sorry, Mike."

Wiping away the tear, I grab my mug, make my coffee, and I decide to head to my front patio to drink my steaming hot cup of goodness and bask in the morning sun; this patio was one of the reasons that I chose this duplex. Just as I sit down, my phone pings with a text.

Mike – *Morning gorgeous*

His text makes me smile but at the same time it breaks my heart. I sit here for ten minutes staring at the screen, typing and deleting, typing and deleting, before finally deciding on what to send him.

Sav – *Morning. Hope you're feeling better **insert photo of my coffee on the patio***

Smiling to myself at sending the pic because I know that Mike hates hospital coffee. *I'm such a bitch*, I giggle to myself as I sip my coffee. Immediately I get a text back.

Mike – *Hope it's scorchin hot...like you*

His reply makes me smile, genuinely smile, and for the first time since it all happened, I feel happy.

It's amazing how Mike has that effect on me, and I like it. But before I take my next breath, reality comes crashing down on me, and I realise the he is currently in hospital because of me...me. As I finish my coffee, I decide that I have to face Mike. I can't keep hiding...even though I love it here in my Sav bubble.

Quickly I shower and change into my denim shorts and white singlet, which I know that Mike likes. I jump in my car and head to the hospital. Along the way, I see Java Lava and decide to stop in to get four coffees, three brownies and one banana bread; I know that Kenz and Jordan will be there, too.

Twenty minutes later, I pull up at the hospital...next to Jordan's Jeep. Smiling to myself when I realise that I know Mike and his friends so well. *It will be hard walking away from them all.*

Grabbing the tray of goodies, I head into the hospital. I'm walking down the corridor towards Mike's room when I see Jordan. He is in the hall trying to soothe Indi. Reaching out, I touch his shoulder and he jumps in fright. Indi groans, and then snuggles back into Jordan.

"Shit, Sav, you scared the crap out of me."

"Sorry, Jordan." I pat Indi on the head and feel she has a bit of a temp, "Is she okay?"

"She's teething at the moment. Today she has a slight temp and is a little grumpy. She's a bit like the patient in there but I'm pretty sure, you are just the medicine that he needs."

Butterflies flap in my stomach when I hear Jordan say this. "How's he doing?"

"He's being a douche again, so I'd say he's back to normal. All going well, he'll be home by the weekend."

"That's awesome. About the home, not the douche part, but then if he wasn't a douche we'd think something was wrong."

"That's true, I wouldn't change him for the world, douchness and all."

We both laugh as I pass him a coffee. "There's also a brownie."

"You're awesome, Sav. Thanks. Go on in and see our patient, he will be happy to see you."

"Thanks, Jordan. See you soon."

Turning, I take a deep breath before hesitantly knocking and slowly pushing the handle down and nudging the door open. When I walk in, both Mike and Kenz look over at me.

Kenz smiles at me, stands up, and walks over to me, with Rory sound asleep in her arms. She gives me a one-armed hug. "Hey, lovely lady," she says and kisses me on the cheek. Grabbing a coffee from the tray, she quietly says, "I'm going to check on Jor, back in a sec." She winks at me as she quietly closes the door. I know she doesn't care about Jordan, well she does, but at the moment she just wants to give us some privacy.

Looking towards the bed, I see that Mike is staring at me intently, his gaze wandering over my body. Pausing at my boobs, before he looks directly into my eyes. The corner of his lips lifts into a sexy grin; his stunning blue eyes are bright and filled with desire and lust. The butterflies from before take flight again, and a slight pink tinge overtakes my cheeks.

"Hey, Mike," I shyly say as I walk over to the bed, placing the coffee and food bag on the bed trolley.

"Hey, gorgeous." Leaning forward he grabs a coffee and looks in the bag. "What do we have here?" He pulls out the brownies and banana bread and groans in delight. "Oh My God! Sav, you are the best. I've been dying, the coffee here tastes like piss and the food is total horseshit.

This here, is the best thing anyone has ever bought me." Taking a sip, he moans, looks back to me, and smiles. "Thanks, you have saved my life, Sav." We both start laughing.

Suddenly I remember that he's in a hospital bed... because of me. I stop laughing and look directly at him. Seriously I say, "If it wasn't for me, you wouldn't be drinking piss flavoured coffee, eating shitty food, or be lying in a hospital bed." Tears begin pouring down my face. Through my sobs I manage to say, "It's because of me you're here." **SNIFF** "I'm so so sorry, Mike."

Climbing out of bed, he walks over and wraps his arms around me, hugging me close to his chest. He whispers quietly, "Shhhh."

Rubbing my back in circles to soothe me, he pulls back, placing a hand on each of my cheeks and directs my gaze towards him. "Sav, listen to me. I'm only going to say this once." Pausing for effect, he continues, "It's not you fault, Sav." I try to interrupt him but he shakes his head side to side and places a finger over my lips to silence me. "I do not blame you, if anything I feel like I failed you. I should have protected you better."

Hearing him say that, the floodgates open and I wrap my arms around him. He squeezes me back, and I cry into his shoulder until the door opening interrupts us. Kenz and Jordan come back in and they pause midstep at seeing me falling apart in Mike's arms.

Quickly, I pull back. I can't deal with this at the moment, as I step back from Mike, I close my eyes and say, "There's ahh, umm, brownies and banana bread in the bag. I'll catch you guys later." Turning, I look to Mike and smile. "Glad you're back on your feet, Mike," pausing, I add, "I have to go, take care."

Turning, I quickly exit his room before I make a beeline for the doors and outside. I can hear Kenzie calling after me, but I have to get out of here. I sprint through the car park, climb into my car, and I get out of there as fast as I can.

Halfway home I have to pull over, I can't see thought the tears. I'm struggling to breathe through the sobs. My heart is breaking right now. I know without a doubt that I'm hopelessly in love with Mike, but I can't let go of the guilt, it's eating away at me.

Screaming into the empty car, I thump the steering wheel in frustration. *Chasing Cars* by Snow Patrol plays and I scoff, this song is perfect for my life right at the moment.

Once I've calmed down, I head home, get changed, and head to work. On my way to work, I give Sierra a quick call to get an update; our latest marketing campaign has done amazingly well and profits are up. When I get to work, I jot down a note to give Sierra an amazing bonus. She has done so much for me and I'm so thankful to have her on my team.

Pulling on my apron, I head out and begin work, thankful for the distraction. I'm on autopilot and before I know it, my shift if over and I'm heading home again.

Once home, I change into my PJ's and climb into bed. I lie there, staring at the ceiling, crying. Every time I close my eyes, I think of Mike and how wonderful a life with him could be. Eventually, I cry myself to sleep.

———

For the next week, my life is one continual cycle.

Wake up, think of Mike.

Have my morning coffee, think of Mike.

Go to work, think of Mike.

Come home, think of Mike.

Climb into bed, think of Mike.

Cry in bed while thinking about Mike, before I eventually pass out from crying...and thinking about Mike.

This week has been so hard, not as hard as loosing Mum, Dad, and Jace but a close second. I'm trying my best to erase and ignore Mike from my life, but Mike Mustange is hard to forget. Everywhere I look, I'm reminded of Mike, he's fucking everywhere. Just when I think I'm doing okay, something will happen and my heart breaks all over again.

Mike has been blowing my phone up with texts and calls, but I can't face him. I delete them immediately, not reading or listening to them. Kenz and Jordan have also been texting me, but again, I ignore them, too.

Mike has been into work the past two nights, but thankfully we are doing a stock take at the moment, so I've been working out the back. Jodi has been a trooper and covers the bar for me so I can hide like the big sook that I am.

It's a Friday night, and oddly enough, I have it off; I'm pretty sure Jodi spoke to the boss on my behalf and he gave me the night off. Besides, he knows my head's not in at the moment, and there's a concert on nearby tonight, so we will be super busy. It's better if I'm not there to screw everyone else up...silently, I thank him and Jodi for my night off.

I decide to head to the bottle-o and grab a case of wine, then I decide to stop at the local gourmet deli and buy enough antipasto to feed all of Italy.

I'm sitting on the front patio with my wine and feast when Kenz pulls up. I hold my breath, hoping that she's alone and thankfully, it's just her. She climbs my front stairs and smartassly says, "Well, well, well, what do you know, she is alive after all."

Hearing her say that I start feel guilty, but I also know that I need 'Sav time' to deal with all of this. "I'm sorry, Kenz. I just needed some 'Sav' time."

"Well, that's fair enough, but you could have just texted me that. I've been worried about you, we all have, especially Mike."

She leaves that hanging and I now feel like a total shitty friend. "I'm sorry, Kenz. It's hard to explain right now, but I just feel like a piece of shit for bringing all this onto Mike. I keep thinking, what if it had been me and you the night that my uncle took us?"

"Sav, speaking from a similar but different experience, you can't live with what-ifs. When life hands you lemons, you have two choices. One, you can grab a bottle of tequila and lick, sip, suck. Or two, you squeeze it in your eye and sook in the corner. I know which option I would choose and Sav, I'm pretty sure that I know which option you will go for too. Now, let me put my bottle of wine in the fridge, I'll grab another glass, and we will get this all sorted, once and for all."

Stunned, I sit there and watch Kenz head inside. I'm

shocked at what she said but she's also right. Enough wallowing, I need to get on with my life and not let my uncle bring me down. Fuck that. I'm Savannah Blac and I'm fucking awesome and I deserve to be happy!

44

MIKE

She left; she left without saying a thing, what the fuck? I'm standing there, holding my coffee staring at the door, as it swings closed. I mumble, "She left." Then I shout, "She fucking left!"

Jordan and Kenz are standing there, looking at me and they look as confused as I do. Shaking my head I turn and ask, "What the fuck just happened?"

Kenz is the first to speak, "Mike, I don't know. I can only imagine that she is struggling at the moment. Not only did she have to watch her uncle torture you, but she also found out that he was responsible for the death of her parents and brother."

Snapping my head towards her, I ask, "What the fuck are you talking about? They died in a car accident."

"Mike, her uncle was responsible for that accident, I told you the other day. Don't you remember?"

"This week has been a total blur, but yeah, now I think back, I vaguely remember hearing that. I...I need to go to her, she needs someone right now. She shouldn't be alone at the moment."

Jordan and Kenzie look at each other and smirk, Jordan teases, "Mike loves Sav." And he makes kissing sounds.

Kenz whacks him in the arm, before she starts singing, "Mike and Sav, sitting in a tree, K-I-S-S-I-N-G."

Jordan joins in now, "First comes love; then comes marriage, followed by a baby in a tequila carriage."

We all burst out laughing.

"You two are seriously meant for each other, how did you both know to say tequila carriage?"

In unison...again, they reply, "'Cause we're awesome."

"More like a pair of nutters...but a pair of nutters who were made for each other and that mean the absolute world to me." Pausing, I smile and add, "Seriously guys, I would be lost without you pair, and the past few days have proven that. Thank you for everything."

All of a sudden, I start to sway, side to side, and nearly pass out. Jordan grabs my arm and escorts me back to the bed. Kenz races out and comes back in with the nurse.

Kenz and Jordan leave the room as soon as the doctor arrives, and once again, I'm poked and prodded. They just think I did too much and have requested that I rest. Until I have twenty-four hours without an almost black out, I won't be leaving here anytime soon.

The nurse and doctor leave, so Kenz and Jordan come back in, the girls are getting restless. They say goodbye and promise to be back tomorrow. Now, I'm left alone in my hospital room with my thoughts, and there's only one person on my mind, Savannah Blac. *I need to figure out how to win her over*, I think to myself as I stare out the window.

Sav is pulling away because she feels guilty, she is just like me. If she's not careful, the guilt will eat at her until she is broken; I know, I've been there. I refuse to let that happen to her, she has been through so much already and she deserves happiness. She brought me back to life again, happy-go-lucky Mike Mustange is back. Now it's my turn to return the favour.

I now see light wherever I look, whereas before all I saw was darkness and gloom. I'm free of the guilt over what happened last year, it no longer eats at me, and it's all because of her.

Flicking the hospital room telly on and *Bold* comes on, *winning*. As I'm watching, I keep thinking about Sav. I know I need help and there is only one person who I can ask; Kenz.

Mike – *I need your help winning over Sav!*
Kenz - ***squee** for sure. Wait 'til you get home and we will chat. Rest up...we have a girl to win over*
Kenz - ***squee** I'm soooo fucking excited*

Laughing at her reply, I snort and that only makes me laugh more. *Fuck, I've been hanging around Kenz too much*, I think to myself.

Mike – *Thanks Kenz. You are a rock star*
Kenz – *I know. Night Mike*

I wake the next morning to another text from Kenz

Kenz – *Operation Sav N Mike is a GO!!*
squee*

I laugh at how excited she is, but truth be told, I'm just as excited too. I get another text.

Jordan – *I have your balls here if you want them, loverboy. Kenz told me what you two are up to. You're so whipped. I'm happy for you asshat*
Mike – *Says the whipped one*
Jordan – *Mike's in looooove*

"Bastard!" I mumble to myself out loud, with a huge smile on my face, as it's true, not that I will admit that to the prick.

The door opens, and I'm still wearing my 'pussy ass in love grin' when in walks my doctor and his lackeys, here for morning rounds; fingers crossed I can get out of this joint today.

Looking up I say, "Morning, Doc, so can I haul ass out of here today?"

"Good morning, Mike and no, you still need to be here for a few days yet."

"Doc, I'm fine."

"Mike, you might be fine but you were just tortured,

shot, and unconscious for three days. Your body needs time to recover and from what I'm reading here in your chart, you nearly collapsed just from standing up."

"I wouldn't call it a collapse, I'd say I got caught in a blip in the space time continuum."

"Call it whatever you want, you're not going anywhere, today anyway. Possibly tomorrow, but I'd say the day after that."

"Why are you so mean to me, Doc?"

"You say mean, I say health care professional. Now, lift up your shirt so I can see how the wound is healing, and then I can leave you to annoy the nurses."

The doc leaves and I'm left alone with my thoughts. It's Sav I have on my mind. Grabbing my phone, I text her.

Mike – *Morning gorgeous **insert coffee emoji***

I'm waiting for her reply, but it doesn't come for a few hours. I smile when I grab my phone and see that it's from Sav.

Sav – *Afternoon Mike **insert beer emoji***
Mike – *Sending a beer pic to a dude is hospital is cruel*
Sav – ***pic of tequila bottle and shot glass***
Sav – ***pic of her doing shot***
Mike – *That's hot...and I mean you and not the shot*
Sav – *Thanks. Shots on me when you're out.*

Ohh how I would love to have shots on Sav, I think to myself as another text comes through.

> **Sav** – *Got to get back to work :P Have a goodly nite*
> **Mike** – *I'd love to have shots ON you*
> **Mike** – *Later, gorgeous XO*

I sit staring at me phone; did I really just reply XO in a text? *I'm such a pussy*, I think to myself.

————

Four, long, painful days later, I'm finally released from the hospital. Kenz put her foot down and I'm staying with them for a few days. Even though I have lived on my own since I turned eighteen, she's worried and doesn't trust me on my own.

Actually, I'm not complaining, she has been doting all over me and I'm eating like a king. Jordan and I have beers daily out the back and most of all, I get Mac and Cheese cuddles all day long. There is only one thing missing, Sav.

Sav and I have been texting daily, but she's still holding back. I've asked her if we can meet up in person a few times, but she ignores my request; at least she's texting me. After chatting to Kenz, I've decided to give her space but I'm not letting the string go. Sav and I are meant to be together; we are just like tequila with a beer chaser, perfectly paired.

Seeing Kenz and Jordan together makes me happy and sad. I want that and I want it with Sav; I want to push her but I don't want to scare her off either. It's really hard, like my cock at the moment. I can't even wank because the fucker shot me in my right shoulder and I happen to be right-handed...just my luck.

Tomorrow I have my final check up at the hospital, and if it's all clean, then Kenz will allow to go home. As soon as I get home 'Operation Win Sav' will be put in motion.

45

SAV

MIKE MUSTANGE IS CONSTANTLY ON MY MIND, BUT the guilt I feel outweighs everything else. He keeps asking to meet up and I keep ignoring his request. It's weird, I can text him but when it comes to meeting up or talking on the phone, fear takes over and I just can't do it.

I've asked Kenz to meet me for coffee today at Java Lava, I need her help. I know I told Kenz I'd give it a go with Mike, but I just can't right now. I need to fix me first.

I'm just about to leave and meet Kenz when there is a knock at my door. It's a knock that I haven't heard in a while and it makes me smile. I race to the door; open it up, and standing on the other side is the man of my dreams.

The world around me ceases to exist and all I see is Mike, standing in front of me with a big bunch of sunflowers. "Hi, gorgeous!" He smiles and lifts up the flowers in a cute way.

I'm rooted on the spot, I can't move, my heart is beating erratically. I flick my tongue out and lick my bottom lip, Mike groans. I realise that I'm still just standing there staring. "Hey!" I manage to mumble. "I was just on my way out to meet someone, can I pop over later today?" *Fuck, why did I just say that? I'm not ready to see him yet,* I think to myself.

"I'd love for you to come over later. How about I cook us dinner? I make a wicked lasagna."

"Sounds good, I'll bring a bottle of red." *Fuck, Sav, what are you doing?*

"Awesome, I'll see you later." He leans forwards and kisses me on the cheek, just skimming the edge of my lips, the kiss lingering longer than it should. I close my eyes and savor the moment. before wrapping my arms tightly around him and hugging him close to me.

We stand there hugging each other for a few more moments, before he pulls away. "These are for you, don't forget to put them in water, Sav. I can't wait to see you later." He hands me the flowers before turning and walking down the front steps. When he gets to the bottom, he turns around and says, "By the way, Sav, you look beautiful. See you later."

Standing at the door, I watch him drive away and realise that when I saw him then, I didn't feel as guilty as I normally do. Maybe the time apart is what I needed. Heading inside, I go to the kitchen to put the flowers into a vase.

While I'm filling it with water, a wave of guilt washes over me. I nearly drop and smash the vase, maybe I'm not as okay with this as I thought.

Walking into the café, I see Kenz sitting by the window, waving I head to the counter to order. Once I have my coffee and muffin, I head over to her. "Hey, lovely lady, sorry I'm late." Pausing, I smile as I place everything down, "I...umm...I had an unexpected visitor just as I was leaving." Taking a sip of my coffee, I moan, just as her head snaps up towards me and her eyes are giving me the 'please explain' look.

"Please explain?"

"Ummm, Mike popped over just as I was heading out. He bought be a big beautiful bunch of sunflowers and asked me to go to his place for dinner tonight." Taking another sip, I look up and see Kenz has the biggest smile on her face.

Clapping her hands she excitedly says, "Squee, I'm soooooooo excited for you two. You both deserve all the happiness in the world. I know I don't know you all that well, Sav, but I'm pretty good when it comes to reading people. Well, now days anyway, but that's a whole other story. Anyway, you and Mike are meant for each other. I feel it in my bones."

Smiling, I take another sip of coffee and think about what she just said. "Kenz, I really like, actually, no, I love him." Pausing, I add, "But I feel so guilty; he got shot because of me. How do I erase the guilt of that?"

"I can't answer that, sorry, I'm not that awesome." She winks at me before adding, "But, Mike doesn't seem to care about that and isn't that all that matters?"

"I guess you're right."

"Hell yes, I am. I'm always right, just ask Jordan." We both start laughing, Kenz starts snorting and that sets me off. "Look, Sav, I've never, ever, seen Mike this happy, and you are what makes him happy. Can't you see that?"

"He makes me happy too, deliriously happy."

"I rest my case. Don't let your fear get in the way of your happiness. Everyone deserves to be happy."

The next hour passes quickly and it is nice to just hang and chat; I'm glad that Kenz suggested coffee. We are packing up to go shopping, and find the perfect outfit for tonight, when she runs into her friend, Sarah. She asks if we can take a rain check and I say that's fine. *I'd rather shop alone for what I have in mind.*

Saying hi and bye, I leave the two of them at Java Lava and head off on my shopping expedition.

Three hours later, I'm a few hundred dollars poorer, but I have a cute hot pink halter dress, black wedge sandals, and a sexy black and hot pink *La Senza* strapless bra and undies set.

Heading home, I take a relaxing bath and get ready for my date with Mike.

Tonight is the night that I start living again.

46

MIKE

I've just left Sav's place and now I'm a bundle of nerves. Like I do most times when I'm nervous, or need advice; I head to Jordan's. He knows how to calm me down and he will have amazing beer, too. It's a win/win for me.

When I get there, he's out the back with the girls. They are sitting in their paddling pool, and Jordan is spraying the hose up in the air. They are giggling their cute little heads off when the water droplets hit them. Their laughter is infectious and the nerves I had immediately disappear. I smile; guess Indie and Rory have the same effect on me as Jordan does. "Unky Mike is in da house!" I shout as I scoop down and pick up Rory. *Yes, got the name right.*

"To what do we owe this visit? I'm guessing food or beer?"

"Maybe I just wanted to stop by and say hi, but if you're offering a beer, I won't say no. Can't stay for food, I have a hot date tonight." I wink at him as I put Rory back down and head to the beer fridge to pour us each a stein.

After pouring the beers, I walk over to Jordan and hand him his. He is looking quizzically at me; he takes a sip, swallows, and says, "Okay, what have you done with the sour sack named Mike? When you left here yesterday, you were all heartbroken over Sav and miserable. Now you're all chirpy and have a date."

"Fuck off, I'm not chirpy. Can't a guy just be happy?"

He's still looking at me intently and raises his eyebrows in a 'explain now or I'll kick your ass' kind of way. "If you must know, Sav is coming to my place for dinner tonight." Pausing, I smile when I think about her. "Jordan, I'm in love with her."

"No shit, Sherlock. Blind fire trucking Freddie could have seen that."

"Yeah, well, we all know I'm a tad slow. I know she said she loved me in the hospital, but I'm not sure if she still does."

"Dude, she does."

"Yeah, right. How do you know that?"

"Dude, the way she looks when your name is mentioned is all lovey-dovey." Taking a sip of beer, he adds, "Much like the pussy-whipped look you currently have on your face."

"Fire truck off, butthole." Laughing I add, "That so doesn't have the same effect as saying," lowering my voice I say, "Fuck you, asshole."

Laughing he replies, "Not wrong there, Mike, ohh, how the times have changed."

"Who would have thought your favourite show would be *Octonauts* and that we would swear in code?"

"Pfft, *Ben and Holly's Little Kingdom* is my fav and how the hell do you know what *Octonauts* is?"

"'Cause I'm an awesome uncle, that's why." Just as I say that, both girls squeal in delight. "See, they just confirmed that I'm awesome."

"Dream on, dude. As much as I'd love to hang, I need to get these two down for a nap; otherwise, Kenz will have my balls on a platter if they get overtired. You need to get home and prepare for your big date. What you cooking anyway?"

"Lasagna."

"So, the only thing that you know how to cook?"

"Pretty much. At least I can cook one thing that's edible. There's always Kung Fu Palace if I fire truck it up, but my lasagna is awesome...like me."

"You keep telling yourself that, dude."

"I tell myself that everyday and since I'm awesome, it must work. Do you want a hand to get Mac and Cheese down?"

"Nah, it's all good, Mike, I've got it. Thanks though, you head off home and go get your lovin' on. Hey, why don't the two of you stop by Malt Me tomorrow for lunch? Kenz and I will both be there."

"Sounds like a plan, but let's do a late lunch-early dinner...or even better, a Sunday arv sesh?"

"Sounds good, man, see you then." He scoops up the girls and heads inside. It still amazes me that Jordan has twins.

On the way home, I stop at the shops and get everything to make my famous lasagna. As I'm walking past the jewelers, I see a stunning *Guess* watch in the window. It screams Sav, so I stop and buy it for her.

The lasagna is in the oven cooking and it smells fucking amazeballs. I'm all showered and to calm my nerves, I catch up on the latest episode of *Bold and the Beautiful*. The episode has just finished and there is a knock at the door.

It's show time!

Getting up, I take a deep breath and I walk to the door. Closing my eyes, I take one last breath and grab the handle. When I open the door, my heart rate speeds up when I see Sav, the wind is completely knocked out of me. My eyes travel up and down her body. She's wearing the sexiest dress I have ever seen in my entire life. It's hot pink, and hugs her body perfectly. "Fucking hell, woman, you look stunning."

She smiles and her cheeks turn pink with embarrassment. "Thanks, Mike. You don't look too shabby either."

We are standing in my doorway, just staring and smiling at each other. Both of us grinning like fools. The air around us is electric and I don't want to be anywhere else. "So, can I come in?"

Shaking my head from side to side, to bring myself back to reality, I laugh and say, "Sorry, yeah, ahh, sure. Come on in." Stepping aside, I let her in and watch her ass sashay side to side into my place; my smile increases as I take her in.

She places her handbag and two bottles of wine on the kitchen bench and totally busts me staring at her ass. Smiling at me, she smugly says, "Like what you see?"

"Fuck, yes I do, Sav."

"Wait till you see what's underneath," she says, while suggestively wriggling her eyebrows at me. Turning around and heading into the kitchen, she leaves me standing there stunned and totally turned on. I'm currently sporting a hard-on that would saw through stainless steel.

"Where are the wine glasses?"

Too stunned to talk, I point to the cupboard next to the pantry. She walks over and reaches up to get the glasses. As she reaches up, her dress lifts and gives me a fine view of her toned legs. Closing my eyes, I imagine them wrapped around me, and I can't wait for that to happen later. I walk over to her, wrap my arms around her waist, and she jumps in fright.

After placing the wine glasses down on the bench, she leans back into me and rubs her ass on my growing erection. Tightening my grip, I nibble on her ear before whispering. "I've missed you."

She turns around in my arms and kisses me. Our lips crash together: tongues caressing and exploring, hands roaming and massaging, each of us moaning and groaning as the kiss deepens. Pulling back, she rests her forehead against mine, and breathlessly whispers, "I've missed you, too, Mike."

I'm about to drag her to the bedroom when the timer on the oven goes off. "Saved by the bell," she murmurs.

"More like interrupted," I add, before softly kissing the tip of her nose and turning to check on the lasagna.

Opening the oven, I can smell that it's done, even without checking. Sav moans again and my cock twitches. I think to myself, *Fuck dinner, I just want to sink myself balls deep inside her and make love to her for the rest of my life.* I'm bought back to reality when I hear her beautiful voice. "Mike, that smells amazing."

"Wait till you taste it, not to brag, but my lasagna is to die for."

"You've got tickets on yourself buddy," she says, as she opens the bottle of wine and pours us a glass each.

Grabbing my oven mitts, I sit the lasagna on the stovetop and go to the fridge to get the salad and dressing out. Placing them on the table, I bring the lasagna over just as Sav takes a seat. She looks at everything and smiles. "This all looks amazing, Mike."

"Thanks, Sav," I say, as I place a slice of lasagna on her plate. "Now dig in."

We both serve ourselves salad and fall into comfortable and relaxed conversation. I find myself laughing and really enjoying myself. We both clear the table and she starts to wash up while I pack away the leftovers.

When we have finished, we both head to the lounge. Grabbing her present, I give it to her as I pour us each another wine. Her face lights up when she lifts the lid and she immediately puts in on, I know she's like it. "Mike, I love it, thank you so much." She kisses me on the cheek.

Bending forward, she grabs our glasses. "A toast, to us and our future."

"I'll definitely toast to that."

We clink glasses and then snuggle on the couch together; her head rests on my shoulder. Wrapping my arm around her, I pull her back into my side and rest my palm across her belly. *We fit together perfectly*, I think to myself.

"Thanks for an awesome meal, Mike. You're right; you do cook a wicked lasagna. I do have one question though?"

"Shoot, I'm on open book."

"Why no cucumber in the salad?"

Her question throws me and I start to laugh. "I read a book recently, and this freak does something with a cucumber. Now I just can't bring myself to eat them."

She starts to laugh, like really laugh. Once she has composed herself, she turns, looks me in the eyes and says. "Oh My God! You are such a freak." She leans forward and quickly kisses me. "But you're my freak."

Grabbing her, I flip her onto her back and settle myself between her legs, she squeals in shock and giggles. Pinning her to the couch, I place featherlight kisses up her stomach, across her boobs, and up her neck. I nuzzle and nip my way along her jawline, up to her lips, before kissing her deeply. Sav wraps her arms around my neck, pulling me closer and kisses me back, gently biting on her bottom lip.

Ever so lightly, I run my hands up her sides and she giggles, breaking our kiss. I continue to run my palms towards her breasts when she throws her head back and arches her back. I take the opportunity and cup her perfect tits, squeezing them. She moans my name slowly, "Miiiike!" Grinding her pussy onto my leg as I continue to massage and squeeze her tits. Looking up at me, she whimpers, "I want you, Mike."

RIGHT IN THIS MOMENT, I HAVE NEVER FELT SO loved or been so turned on. I realise that I want Mike Mustange in my life: forever. Looking up at him, I whisper, "I want you, Mike."

Before I can comprehend anything, Mike has lifted me up; I wrap my legs around him. Unapologetically I grind my pussy against his zipper and growing erection, as I continue to kiss him. Carrying me down the hallway towards his room. After placing me on my feet at the end of the bed, he reaches down to grab the hem of my dress, I grab his hand and I say, "No." Stopping in his tracks, he looks hesitantly at me as I push him back onto the bed. Seductively, I whisper, "No, let me. I have a surprise for you."

Stepping back from the bed, I undo the tie on my halter dress and I let it fall down my body, pooling at my feet in a pile of pink chiffon. I'm left standing in my strapless bra and undies; I've never done anything like this before and my heart is rapidly beating. Taking a deep breath, I look at Mike and smile. There is nothing but lust in his big, beautiful blue eyes. His look comforts me and in this moment, I've never felt sexier than I do right now.

I kneel on the end of the bed and slowly shuffle up his body, my breasts rubbing over his crotch. As I straddle him, I lean forward and intensely kiss him, shamelessly grinding my throbbing pussy on his growing erection.

Pulling back, I begin to untuck his shirt. My hands are shaking as I slowly unbutton it. I only get two buttons undone when I give up and tear open his shirt, buttons flying everywhere. He looks up at me in shock. "In a hurry, sweetness? 'Cause I can tell you now, I ain't going anywhere...anytime soon."

"Sorry, I don't know what came over me. I'll buy you a new shirt."

"I don't care about the shirt, now come here and kiss me, woman."

Leaning forward, I kiss him before pulling back. "Don't ever call me 'woman' again." Leaning down, I kiss him intently.

"Yes, ma'am," he says in between kisses.

"Last chance, Mike Must..." He cuts me off by kissing me senseless.

Flipping me onto my back again, he deepens our kiss, pinning me to the bed. He begins to massage my tits, and unashamedly I grind my pussy against him.

Our kiss is so deep, so hungry, and so erotic that it brings me to orgasm; my body trembling and tingling as the pleasure courses through my veins. "Holy fucking shitballs. I've heard of a kissgasm before but I've never experienced one until now," I murmur to myself, as my body and mind come back to reality.

Opening my eyes, I see Mike staring intently at me. "Did you just come?"

Sheepishly, I say, "Yep, I just had my first kissgasm."

"Well, I'm glad I was your first, Sav. Now let's see if I can bring you 'O' number two for the evening."

Before I have a chance to reply, Mike is kissing me again, our hands roaming over each other's bodies. One-handedly, he undoes my bra and flicks it across the room before making quick work of my undies.

I'm lying completely naked on his bed, and I see that he still has his pants on. "Umm, I think you are over-dressed, mister."

"I can fix that." He quickly jumps up and removes his pants and boxer briefs in one quick motion, and then jumps back on the bed. "Is that better, milady?"

"Much, now do dirty, wonderful things to my body...please?"

"With pleasure."

His lips are on mine instantaneously and his kiss almost brings me to orgasm again. Before I can get there, he kisses his way down my neck and chest. Taking one of my nipples into his mouth, he gently bites down on the tight bud before sucking it deeply into his mouth. I moan in delight, "Fuck, I love your mouth."

He replies by licking, sucking, and nipping my other breast.

His hand snakes its way down my stomach towards my core, inching closer and closer to my throbbing pussy; I'm eagerly awaiting his magic fingers. Just as he reaches the top of my slit, he snakes his hand back up my stomach and massages my breast before rolling and squeezing the nipple between his fingers.

Grabbing his hand, I guide it down my body and together we explore my wet folds. Our fingers simultaneously rubbing circles around my clit, before sliding down my slit and plunging deep inside of me; in and out, deeper and deeper. I'm so worked up that it doesn't take long until I'm once again tumbling over the edge as our fingers continue to dance together, deep inside of me.

Kissing me deeply, he pulls back and whispers, "That's two."

Falling back onto the bed, closing my eyes, I whisper, "Mmhmm!" My breathing is still returning to normal, when I feel Mike run the tip of his finger up my stomach, drawing circles around my breasts. It tickles and I laugh, swatting his hand away. "Mike, stop! That tickles."

"Is this better?" He seductively states before sucking my nipple into his mouth and gently biting down on my sensitive tip. Releasing my nipple, I sigh at the loss of contact. "You have gorgeous tits, Sav. I could suck and fuck them all day long...forever even."

Looking up at him, I smile. "Well, what are you waiting for, Mike? Fuck my tits."

"Abso-fuckin-lutely nothing."

He crushes his lips to mine in a deep sensual kiss that invokes all these feels and pulses in all the good places. Eventually, we come up for air and he straddles my stomach. Reaching out, he gently massages my tits before pushing them together. He nudges the tip of his cock between them. Mike begins thrusting between my tits, I've never done this before but it feels amazing.

The tip of his cock pokes through the top of my tits and I get an idea. On the next thrust, I lift my head and dart my tongue out to lick the tip, continuing this until I hear him say, "Suck me, Sav, I'm gonna come."

Leaning forward, he shoves his cock deep into my mouth and I suck hard while I fondle his balls. Once I have sucked him dry, I look up into his eyes and see him intently staring back at me. "That's one for you, baby."

"Well, it seems like you are slightly winning, let's see if we can increase your lead." Before I know it, his cock is lined up with my entrance and he is teasing me. Gently inching in and then pulling back out again, he does this over and over. I feel like I'm about to explode when he thrusts deep inside of me.

"Fuuuuck!" I shout out as he keeps slamming into me.

Lifting my hips, I meet him thrust for thrust. I place my feet on the bed and lift my hips; he grips me tight and continues his assault on my pussy. "I'm close, Mike."

He grunts, "Let go, Sav. Coat me with your pussy juices." That's sets me off like a rocket. My pussy clenches around him and I explode around his cock. My whole body tingles as he continues to thrust into me. The pleasure is never-ending; I never want this feeling to end. I feel his cock harden and his body tenses as his orgasm rips through him.

Falling on top of me, he nuzzles my neck before whispering, "That's three, baby."

Wrapping my arms around him, I laugh and reply. "That's two for you."

"Baby, this isn't about me. I get just as much pleasure watching you come. Actually, it's my new favourite thing to watch."

"Even better than *Bold*?"

"So fucking better, Sav."

He rolls off me and we snuggle into each other, my back to his front. Neither of us says a word but the silence says it all. Just before I fall asleep, I hear him whisper, "I'm going to marry you one day, Savannah Blac."

48

MIKE

LIFE COULD NOT BE BETTER. SAV AND I ARE OVER THE moon happy, and we have decided to move in together. We are pretty much joined at the hip and financially it makes more sense. Not that she needs to worry about money, considering she's a bazillionaire and all.

We found an amazing cottage, just out of the city, so I only have a small commute each day. Plus, it's just around the corner from the Dungeon; we wanted something near the bar as it's our place and holds a special meaning to us both. Sav quit her bartending job and now works from home, remotely running the jewelry stores so it didn't bother her too much where we lived.

"Sav, that was the realtor. The settlement cheque from the bank cleared, the cottage is officially ours."

She comes barreling down her hallway and jumps into my arms, wrapping her legs around my waist, and kissing me hard. Breaking our kiss, she pulls back and with a megawatt smile excitedly declares, "Squee, I'm so excited to be moving in with you. I love you, Mike Francine Mustange."

"Seriously, give up on the middle name thing. If Kenz ever finds out, she will hand me my balls on a silver platter with the teasing. I refuse to let that happen."

"Okay, Mike Francine Mustange, I will stop saying, Mike Francine Mustange, just as soon as you kiss me."

"I will happily kiss you anytime, Sav, and now that we will be living together, I will kiss you anytime I want."

"We just bought a cottage," she squeals with excitement.

Lowering her down onto the chaise, I cover her body with mine, and kiss her deeply. She wraps her arms around my neck and begins to grind her pussy on my leg. Lifting up, I run my hand up her skirt and rub her folds through her undies.

Closing her eyes she moans, pushing her pussy against my fingers. Her breathing becomes faster, and she lifts her shirt up and starts massaging her tits through her silky, satin, pink bra. Her moans are getting louder, and just as she's ready to explode, I pull back and stand up. Looking down at her, I smirk. "Come on, babe, we need to go meet Amanda and get our keys."

She lies there, open-mouthed, staring at me. "Are you fucking kidding me?"

I chuckle as I reach over and drag her to the edge of the chaise. Quickly, I lift her skirt, pull her undies to the side and attack her pussy. Licking, sucking, and nibbling, I dine on her delectable pussy, bringing her to climax with my tongue only. Screaming my name out in pleasure, she explodes all over my face, drowning me in my second favourite drink.

Pulling back, I wipe my chin and smile. "Now that I've had breakfast, we can go."

Sitting up, she pulls me in tight and kisses me. "I love tasting myself on you. Now, let's go get our keys so we can christen the new place."

"Fuck, I love you and your wicked, dirty mind. Now, grab the tequila in the kitchen and let's go."

Forty minutes later, after all the I's are dotted and the T's are crossed, we are officially homeowners. Amanda has just left and Sav and I are standing in our lounge room, taking it all in.

"Can you believe it, baby? This is all ours." I outstretch my arms and spin like that nun chick from *The Sound of Music*.

"Mike, I'm soo unbelievably happy right now." Smiling over at me, she grabs the hem of her shirt, and strips it off, before quickly removing her skirt, leaving her standing there in just her bra.

"Umm, where are your undies?"

"In the bathroom," she says, staring at me as she runs her fingers down her stomach towards her pussy, which is glistening wet.

Stalking over to her, I grab her wrist. "Uhh, uh, Sav. That's my pussy." Getting onto my knees, I hook her leg over my shoulder and slide my tongue up and down her slit. We both groan in delight. "Fuck, I love eating your pussy." Continuing to suck and lick her slit before adding a finger, I feel her pussy walls tighten and just before she's about to come, I pull away, and she whimpers. "Sav, the first time you come in our new house, I will be balls deep inside of you."

Quickly I remove my clothes and Sav jumps into my arms. She wraps her legs around my waist, and I thrust deep inside of her before pushing her against the TV wall; I continue to thrust into her. We are both moaning in delight and together we crash over the edge, crying out each other's names as we draw out each other's pleasure. Spinning around, I slide down the wall with Sav still in my arms.

Looking deep into her eyes, I lean forward and take her lips in a deep, sensual kiss. "Thank you, Sav."

"Why are you thanking me?"

"You made me whole again, Sav. I never thought I would be this deliriously happy, and I have you to thank for that."

Wiping a tear away, she says, "Mike, I feel exactly the same. I've never ever been this happy and it's all because of you. I love you, Mike 'I promise never to say Francine again' Mustange"

"I love you too, Savannah Blac."

———

A week later on Friday night, I'm on my way home from work and I decide to stop at the bottle-o to get some wine for Sav. Ss I'm walking out, there's a lady doing a tequila tasting, and I just have to stop and taste. Oh My God! I taste the smoothest tequila that I've had in a long-time. It's almost as good as the bottle the Kenz and Jordan bought back from Mexico for me, so I grab a bottle and head to the checkout...tonight is going to be amazeballs.

When I get in my car, I send off a quick text to Sav.

Mike – *On my way home...I have a surprise*

Immediatly I get a reply.

Sav – *I have a surprise too...hurry*
Mike – *Be there in 5*

I'm intrigued to see what surprise Sav has for me. Luck unfortunately isnt on my side this evening; I get every red light on the way home and to top it off, I get stuck due to an accident.

Mike – *Stuck in traffic*
Sav – *Bugger...looks like I'll just start without you*
Sav - ***picture of her shoulder, bra strap down and a hint of purple lace covering boobs***
Mike – *You don't play fair*
Sav - ***picture of bed, candles and her leg***
Sav – *But you love me anyway...hurry home Xo*
Mike – *Considering parking car and running home. Traffic starting to flow, be there soon*
Sav – *Can't wait **SMOOCHES***

Just my luck that this would happen, Sav is such a little minx...I can't wait to get home now.

Thankfully, I pass the accident quickly and by the looks, no one was seriously hurt. From this point on, I get green ligths all the way and I'm home in no time.

Sav and I moved into our cottage last weekend and there are boxes everywhere; some are unpacked, some half unpacked, but most are still taped up. Neither of us can be assed unpacking.

Parking my car, I walk inside, dump my bag by the door, and head to the kitchen to put the wine in the fridge. After putting the wine away, I search out two shot glasses, and then I will search for Sav.

I'm bent over in a box when Sav comes up behind me, wraps her arms around me, and seductivey whispers, "Evening, sexy."

Rubbing my hands over her arms, I stand up and spin around. My mouth drops open at the vision in front me me. Sav is standing there in my favourite bra and undie set; it's a deep purple satin and it pushes up her girls magnificanlty.

"Evening yourself." My eyes dart up and down her body. "Fuck, Sav, you are so sexy."

Her cheeks turn a shade of pink and she looks towards the floor all shy. Reaching out with my index finger, I lift her chin so she is looking directly at me. "Don't hide from me, gorgeous." Bending forward, I place a kiss on the tip of her nose an she smiles. "You can't hide from me, I'll find you everytime."

Turning around, I grab the tequila, turn back to Sav and wink. "So, I thought tonight we could have some tequila fun."

Sav bursts out laughing. "Did you stop at the bottle-o

on Stanley Street?"

"Yeah, why?"

She turns towards the lounge and returns with the same bottle of tequila, holding it up, she smiles and says, "Great minds think alike." She winks and then walks back into the lounge.

With her back towards me, I stalk over to her, wrap my arms around her waist and lift her up; she squeals and starts laughing. Gently I lower her to the couch, flip her over, and cover her body with mine. Grabbing her cheeks in my hands, I kiss her deeply, slipping my tongue into her mouth. I close my eyes and loose myself in kissing her. Sav wraps her arms around me and pulls me closer to her.

Reluctanly, I pull away, break the kiss, and head to the kitchen. Grabbing the salt and precut limes, I head back to the lounge. Sav is still laying on the couch, her cheeks flushed and lips swollen; my cock hardens at the sight before me. "Fuck me, Sav. You are absolutely gorgeous."

Her cheeks become a shade darker and she smiles at me seductively. She runs a finger from her chin, down her neck, before circling it across the edge of her bra.

Straddling her hips, I lean forward and kiss her quickly before I lick down the path that her finger just took. I wink at her as I grab the salt and shake it along the line I just left. Ripping the cap off the tequila, I take a swig and sigh; *this shit is amazeballs*. Placing the bottle over Sav's mouth, she opens, and I pour the tequila into her mouth. A few drops spill down her chin, leaning forward I lick the tequila and salt off her before kissing her deeply again. The salt and tequila combining as our mouths mesh together. Pulling away, I grab the lime and suck, while the lime juice is still on my lips, I kiss Sav again. She sucks my bottom lip into her mouth and moans. "Man, that tequila is amazing," she lustifuly says, as she reaches for the bottle and takes another swig before handing the bottle to me. I take it from her and place it on the coffee table.

Pulling Sav into my arms, I kiss her again and undo the clasp on her bra, flicking it across the room. Pushing her back to the couch, I kiss and lick my way down her body, twirling my tongue in her navel as I kiss my way down her stomach. I kiss her mound through the satin before nudging it aside and licking her clit. Sav moans and lifts her hips, allowing me to remove her undies.

Grabbing the tequila, I pour it on her stomach and quickly lick the spills so I don't ruin our new couch, but right at this moment, I don't give a flying fuck about it. As I'm licking the spills, Sav shakes the salt on her stomach, grabs a piece of lime and places it between her lips. Licking the salt, I suck the tequila from her belly button before kissing my way up her stomach and neck; finally I suck the lime and kiss Sav. She brazenly grinds herself on me as I continue to kiss her. Pulling back, I remove the lime rind and kiss her deeply.

My cock is rock hard and Sav reaches down and rubs me through my jeans; I'm so turned on that I grab her hand. "If you keep that up, I'm going to blow in my jeans and I haven't done that since I was fifteen."

Sav looks up at me and smiles. "Fuck me, please."

She knows I can't resist her so I lean back, unbutton

my jeans, and quickly remove them and my shirt. In one swift motion, I'm balls deep inside of Sav; she's so wet that I easily slide in and out of her.

Without warning, I flip us so she is on top. Reaching out, I massage her tits, and she gets up on her knees and begins to ride me. Throwing her head back in ecstasy, she slides up and down my throbbing cock. Sav entwines her fingers with mine and together we massage and rub her gorgeous breasts.

This is my favoiurite position, I can get deep inside of Sav and I love to watch her unfold in front of me. Sav continues to play with her tits as I grip her hips and meet her thurst for thrust. I feel her pussy walls tighten around my cock. She stills as her orgasm rips through her body and screams my name; her head thrown back and eyes closed as she comes back to earth. She continues to ride me until my legs tighten and I explode, tumbling over the edge, emptying myself deep inside of her.

Opening my eyes, I look up to see Sav staring down at me with a sated smile on her face. "Definitely, the best tequila ever," she says as she lies on top of me.

"Definiely a good drop," I say before wrapping my arms tightly around her. "I love you, Savannah Blac."

"I love you too, Mike Francine Mustange."

I'm too content to say anything about the use of the middle name. It's in this moment, I realise that I am the happiest I have ever been, and it's all due to the amazing woman lying in my arms.

THE END!

EPILOGUE

Mike

LOOKING AROUND, I SEE THAT EVERYONE IS HAPPY and having fun. For the first time, in a long time, I realise that I'm at a party having fun along with everyone, too. I owe my happiness to Sav. She bought me back to life and I could not be happier.

It was a rough ride to get here, and after the events of last year, I didn't think I would ever be happy, or in love again. I now know that there is a difference between what you think is love and what is deep, heartfelt, unconditional love; and that's what I have with Sav. She came along when I least expected it, but I'm happy she did. I have never been happier.

Luckily, I also have great friends who helped me pull my head in and be the happy-go-lucky me again. Without the support and guidance of Kenz and Jordan, I don't know where I would be. I know that had they not intervened after my property getaway, I wouldn't be here. I would have drank myself to death, and then I wouldn't have met Sav and taken a chance with her

Kenz was right, not that I will ever tell her that. It wasn't my fault that my crazy ex was related to her psycho ex. They had a plan, and we were the unfortunate pawns caught in the middle of their sick and twisted vendetta, Kenz more so than anyone. If she can overcome it, I can too; after all, I'm Mike Francine Mustange, and I have the most amazing woman now living with me.

Sav and I have officially moved in together and today is our housewarming. Everyone who is near and dear to Sav and me are here today to help us celebrate, and I've arranged a super surprise for her. I can't wait for it to get here.

Sav and I are always doing little things for each other. Leaving love notes in random spots, but our fav thing to do is leave miniatures of tequila lying around. Trying to explain away a miniature in your work briefcase was fun, but thankfully my boss knows how crazy Sav and I are, and it was brushed aside. After that, we set some ground rules and boundaries for our games.

A lot can occur in twelve months, but what I've come to realise is that shit happens, some shit you can control and some shit is beyond your control. It's how you deal with it that proves the person you are.

Sav and I were destined to find each other, we are polar opposites with most things, but we also bring out the best in each other. I can unequivocally say, she saved me. I love her with all my heart; she's not only the one, she's my savior. Sav gave me a reason to live and smile again. I'm one lucky son of a bitch. One of these days, I will make Sav my wife, but in the meantime, we will enjoy tequila and each other...sometimes together.

Sav

It's amazing the difference twelve months can make. Twelve months ago, I was still living at home with Mum, Dad, and Jace and plodding along. Now, I'm an orphan, living with the man of my dreams and I'm over the moon happy. I just wish that Mum, Dad and Jace could have met Mike.

Mike rescued me from an existence that was getting me down and bought me back to life. Prior to meeting Mike, I was existing, just plodding along and not living. Uncle Kelvin didn't help things, but with Mike's help, I overcame that obstacle and I'm now living life to the fullest.

I know that Mum, Dad, and Jace would be so happy for me. My heart still aches for them, but Mike has helped fill that void. Our road to happiness has been bumpy but I wouldn't change a thing; well, maybe the kidnapping. I'd give up that but everything that has happened has led me to this point...to Mike.

Looking over at Mike, I smile to myself. He is just as happy as I am, and I love him to the moon and back. Mike brings out the best in me. He is always doing little things to surprise me, but his latest gift was beyond amazing. He arranged for my best friend from home, Logan to be here.

It has been so great catching up with him, I didn't realise how much I missed our friendship.

Arms wrap around my waist and tickle me, jumping in fright; I turn around and whack Logan in the arm. "Fuck, you're such an asshole. I didn't miss that."

"Naw, come on, Sav, you totally missed me."

"Maybe," I say as I sip on my wine.

"There's no maybe, baby, you were miserable until we started chatting again, and when I told you that I was here, your life was complete."

"Pfft, you keep telling yourself that. Pretty sure my happiness is standing over there doing shots, but yes, I am excited to have you back in my life again. I missed you like crazy. I can't believe you've been here all this time. By the way, I can't wait to see your new penthouse."

"You only want me for my penthouse."

"Yes. You got me. I knew at age ten that by age twenty-seven you'd have a penthouse, and that's why I ran you over with my pushie."

"See, told you." We both burst out laughing. "Seriously, Sav, it's good to see you smiling again. I was so worried about you. Before you left, you were distant and not just because you lost your family. I was hurting for you, I wanted to do more but you wouldn't reach out or let anyone in. Then you took off without warning, that gutted me, Sav."

"I'm sorry I did that, so sorry, Loge. I thought I was doing the right thing." Pausing, I take a sip and add, "You're here now, and I met Mike, so in a way it all worked out. Don't you think?"

"I'll let you have that one, but if you ever take off again like you did, it will be on like Donkey Kong."

"Promise, I'm not going anywhere."

"Except to the bar."

"Dude, when are you going to realise that I'm..."

Mike walks over, puts his arm around my shoulder, pulls me in tight and interrupts, "The sexiest woman here."

Logan laughs, "And that's my cue to leave." He turns around and pauses midstep.

————

Sarah

I'm really not in the mood for a party tonight, but I can't keep ignoring everyone. Just because my life sucks, doesn't mean I should take it out on my friends. Hanging up from Kenz, who is making sure I'm coming, for the fifth time today; I grab my car keys, take a deep breath, and head off.

When I arrive at Mike and Sav's, a pang of jealousy overtakes me at how stunning their cottage is. Seeing all this makes me miss having my own place. Don't get me wrong, I love the apartment that I'm currently in, but it's not mine. As usual, my life turns to shit just when everyone else's seems to be taking off.

Finding Mike and Sav, I offer my congrats before seeking out Kenz. Of course, she's by the bar holding a glass of wine out for me. "Well, well, well, look, Jor, it's

Sarah. You remember her? My bestie who seems to have disappeared off the face of the Earth."

"Hardy har har, bitch." I hug them both. "It's good to see you guys." Turning to Kenz, I look at her with puppy dog eyes that I know will get her. "Kenz, I'm sorry I've been such a shitty friend, but I promise, I'll explain everything...soon."

"You know I can't resist your puppy dog eyes, so I'll give you a pass...for now, but you and I will be talking; soon."

"I know, I know, and I promise that I will but for tonight, I'm going to get rip-roaring drunk with my besties and have a winetabolous time." Taking the glass of wine from Kenz, I yell, "Cheers!" and clink glasses with her.

Chugging it back, I ask for another when I hear a voice that makes me tingle all over. Spinning around, I see him, standing there talking to Sav and Mike. He has his back to me, but I'd know him from a mile away.

I'm still staring when he turns around, our eyes lock across the room, he pauses midstep and smiles. A force takes over my body and I find myself walking towards to him, his pull is too strong to ignore.

He is standing directly in front, staring intently at me, he says, "Sarah?" His sexy baritone voice completely melts me.

The room is dead silent, everyone is looking at us but they all fade away. It's just Logan and me, standing there, totally absorbed in one another; the air around us is filled with lust, sexual tension, and confusion.

Finding my voice, I stammer. "LLL...Logan, what are you doing here?"

"Sav's the friend I mentioned. What are you doing here?"

Once again I'm frozen, unable to speak. Everything I have been hiding is about to unravel, and the biggest secret of all is standing right in front of me. All six foot two inches of gorgeousness. "I...I...I have to go." Turning, I race towards to front door, slamming it behind me.

Leaning against it, I stand there hyperventilating, trying to catch my breath. I can hear chatter behind the door but the only voice I focus on is his, I here him say, "That's the girl I was telling you about, Sav."

Sliding down the door, I start to cry, my world is beginning to crumble...again.

Read on for a sneak peek at Wine Not, Book 3 in the
Liquor Cabinet Series.

PROLOGUE

It's so good to hang out with Kenz, Jordan, and Mike
again and to finally get to know Sav. I'm glad that Kenz
kept pestering me to come, I think I need to spend more
time with them so I don't lose myself down the rabbit
hole that I'm currently stuck in. It's hard keeping it all
hush-hush, but the focus is on Mike and Sav tonight so
my secret will be safe...for now.

After a rough trot, things are looking up for Mike and
Sav, they are extremely happy and recently bought a
gorgeous cottage together, hence the housewarming
party. I'm still amazed that Mike has fallen in love and
with a gazillionaire. His girlfriend, Sav, is the sole owner
of Blac Family Jewellers. If you had told me twelve
months ago that Mike would be all domesticated and
have a girlfriend, I would have told you to put down the
crack pipe. Mind you, I didn't expect my life to end up
the way it has either.

"So, Sarah, where have you been hiding?" Jordan
asks, as he hands Kenz and me another wine.

"Ummm, work, I literally live there at the moment."
Which isn't a complete lie. "Mmm, this wine is heaven.
It's so fruity but not too sweet, really refreshing."

Kenz looks at me and smiles. "Sarah, you totally need
to become a wine critic, or even better open a wine bar.
I'd have a beer hubby and a wine bestie."

"You front the mullah and I'll totally do that." As I

take a sip, I think of a recent conversation I had regarding this, *maybe I should take the leap*; it would get me away from 'her.' Taking another sip, I cheekily reply, "I can see it now, the bar would be broke in a week 'cause the owner's bestie drank all the stock."

"Pfft, if I haven't drunk the brewery dry yet, I doubt I could do it to your bar." Winking at me she adds, "But I'm totally up for the challenge."

"I have a better idea, me and you run the wine bar together, like we used to talk about when we were at school, and we will become wineaires."

"What the hell is a wineaire?"

"Like a billionaire, but with wine."

Kenz slings her arm over my shoulder. "And this is why I missed you so much. You take my shit and turn it into an idea that would work."

Laughing, Jordan says, "If you two ran a bar, it would be broke before the end of the first day. Nope, not gonna happen for you, Kenz." She pouts at him, so he pulls her into his side and kisses her gently head. Looking back at me, he points with his finger that's wrapped around his beer mug. "I can totally see you doing that though, Sarah."

"Naw thanks, Jordan, but I doubt anyone would give me the capital to start it." Looking at Kenz, I poke my tongue and say, "Suck it, Kenz, your husbut likes me better than you." As I take another sip of wine, my mind drifts off to my imaginary wine bar. *I would totally love to do that, but before that can happen, I need to get my life back on track*, I think to myself.

She punches me in the arm really hard. "Pfft, what-evs, Bitch."

Magically, I don't spill a drop. "Winning!" I proudly declare fist pumping the air and lifting my leg in a slight kick to the side as I do so. Both Jordan and Kenz clap when all of a sudden my skin prickles. I freeze on the spot. I feel his presence, but it can't be him. Turning around, I scan the room, and then I see him standing over near Mike and Sav, looking ever so sexy in jeans and a button-down shirt.

My heart is racing and I swallow hard just as he turns around, our eyes lock onto one another. All that I have been hiding these past few months is all about to unravel, due to the demigod standing in front of me. I'm going to be exposed; No, No, No...Oh My God, I can't believe he's here, this can't be happening.

I'm fucked...my secret is about to be exposed.

Wine Not, Book 3 in the Liquor Cabinet Series is now available.

ACKNOWLEDGMENTS

Once again, I need to thank my hubby and kids for encouraging me to do this and for putting up with me ignoring you when I was in the zone or in edits. A special shout out to Piper, your words of encouragement along the way are beautiful, just like you. Also, thanks for handing out bookmarks and pimping mummy's books.

To the following authors for your guidance on the writing path; **Jodi Perry, Anita Gillham, Lyssa Layne, Elle Brookes, BJ Harvey, Amo Jones, Angel Justice, Elizabeth Wells, Rebecca Rohman** and **Michele Stratton.** Thank you from the bottom of my heart, this authoring is hard and your help is greatly appreciated. A special thank you also goes out to the peeps in Sprint City group, your sprinting helps me reach my deadlines and I appreciate the encouragement.

To my beta readers **Amanda, Amy, Beth, Heather, Megan, Patti** and **Sierra** thank you for taking the time to read Tequila Healing and for giving me your honest feedback and suggestions, I really appreciate it.

My editor **Karen**, thank you again for taking the time to turn my baby into something amazing. One of these days I'll get the punctuation perfect the first time...I hope. And I will have you speaking Aussie in no time at all. From the bottom of my heart, thank you Karen for all that you do.

My mum, **Helen Marshall**, for proof reading Tequila Healing. Your praise and words of encouragement mean the world to me. I know you don't like the "silly scenes" but I'm sure you will be fine, after all you have read Jodi and Lili's books.

Tash Drake from **Outlined with Love Designs**, you designed me a cover that was perfect for Mike and Sav. I love working with you and am happy to have you on my team.

A special thank you **Elizabeth Wells** for allowing me to reference your series within my book and for your guidance, support and encouragement throughout the writing process.

PSST. Her books can be found online #JustSayin and they really are awesome.

Thanks **K Webster** for allowing me to reference the cuce; I will never ever look at a cucumber the same again. Also for helping me get the spelling of a word correct.

...and lastly, **you, the reader**. Thanks for reading Tequila Healing, I hope you love Mike and Sav just as much as I do.

TEQUILA HEALING PLAYLIST

Sexual Healing – Marvin Gaye
Money For Nothing – Dire Straits
Stand by Me – The Drifters
Numb – Linken Park
These Days – Powderfinger
Closer – Nine Inch Nails
Hot N Cold – Katy Perry
Coming Undone – Korn
Leave Me Alone – Natalie Imbruglia
The Sound of Silence – Disturbed
So What – Metallica
Sober P!nk
Bye Bye Beautiful – Nightwish
Hey Hey, My My – Battleme
Forever Young – Audra Mae & The Forest Rangers
John the Revelator – Curtis Stigers
Slipkid – Anvil
Girl from the North Country – The Lions
Bring Me to Life – Evanescence

Hero – Enrique Iglesias
Bad Romance – Lady Gaga
Sweet Disposition – The Temper Trap
Monster – Skillet
Broken – Seether
Get Lucky – Daft Punk feat. Pharell Williams
Sex on Fire – Kings of Leon
Supermassive Black Hole – Muse
Little Lion Man – Mumford & Sons
To Be Alone – Hozier
Carry on Wayward Son – Kansas
Better – The Scream Jets
Heroin Girl – Everclear
Highway to Hell – AC/DC
You've Got Time – Regina Spektor
Chasing Cars – Snow Patrol
I Want to Know What Love Is – Foreigner

This playlist can be found on Spotify.

https://open.spotify.com/user/1254969568/
playlist/3RnjQ2EewzWfU9TyLEk1Mx

ABOUT THE AUTHOR

DL Gallie is from Queensland, Australia, but she's lived in many different places all over the world, including the UK and Canada. She currently resides in Central Queensland with her husband and two munchkins. She and her husband have been together since she was sixteen, and although they drive each other crazy at times, she couldn't imagine her life without him.

Shortly after her son was born, DL began reading again. With encouragement from her husband, she picked up the pen and started writing, and now the voices in her head won't shut up.

DL enjoys listening to music, drinking white wine in the summer, red wine in the winter, and beer all year round. She's also never been known to turn down a cocktail, especially a margarita.